Little Green Men

Book, Music and Lyrics by
Scott Martin

A SAMUEL FRENCH ACTING EDITION

SAMUEL
FRENCH
FOUNDED 1830

NEW YORK HOLLYWOOD LONDON TORONTO

SAMUELFRENCH.COM

ISBN 978-0-573-69858-3   Printed in U.S.A.   #29652

RENTAL MATERIALS

An orchestration consisting of a **Piano/vocal score, 13 vocal chorus books, Conductor's score, Clarinet/Saxophone, Rhythm Guitar, Drums/Percussion, and Bass** will be loaned two months prior to the production ONLY on the receipt of the Licensing Fee quoted for all performances, the rental fee and a refundable deposit. Additionally, a music-only performance **Accompaniment CD** and **Sound Effects CD** (including edited Charlie McCarthy and *War of the Worlds* radio cues) is available for rental.

Please contact Samuel French for perusal of the music materials as well as a performance license application.

IMPORTANT BILLING AND CREDIT REQUIREMENTS

All producers of *LITTLE GREEN MEN must* give credit to the Author of the Play in all programs distributed in connection with performances of the Play, and in all instances in which the title of the Play appears for the purposes of advertising, publicizing or otherwise exploiting the Play and/or a production. The name of the Author *must* appear on a separate line on which no other name appears, immediately following the title and *must* appear in size of type not less than fifty percent of the size of the title type.

In addition the following credit *must* be given in all programs and publicity information distributed in association with this piece:

LITTLE GREEN MEN was developed with the generous cooperation and support of John Sparks and the Academy for New Musical Theatre; www.anmt.org

LITTLE GREEN MEN was first produced by Calia Mintzer and Larry Cosgrove for the Kentwood Players at the Westchester Playhouse in Westchester, California on September 12, 2008. The performance was directed by Scott Martin, choreographed by Alison Matizza, with sets by Tony Pereslete; costumes by Sheridan Cole Crawford, Jayne Hamil, and Shirley Hatton; lighting by Tom Brophey; sound by Susan Stangl; set decoration and creature design by Valerie Ruel; and props by Judy Polak. The production stage managers were Jordan Bland and Adam Dunberger. The cast was as follows (in order of appearance):

TED CONNORS.	Drew Fitzsimmons
IDA ROTHBERG	Marcy Agreen
SPARKY SCHULTZ	Sergio Christophalo
NANCY GRIBBLE	Francesca Palermo
CARL BENNETT	Slater Garcia
JOAN McDOOGLE	Megan Moylan
JOEY DeLUCA.	Dylan LaRocque
GEORGIE JOHNSON	Logan Gould
MARY GALE.	Hannah Provisor
SUSIE SLAUSON	Emma Kate Hatton
MRS. KOLOSTKY	Susan Goldman Weisbarth
MORTY KLEIN	Greg Abbott
SALLY DUNBAR	Meredith M. Sweeney

ADDITIONAL PRODUCTION CREW:

Assistant Directors.	Jayne Hamil, Sheridan Cole Crawford
Recording Engineer	Devin Thomas
Master Carpenter	Lori A. Marple-Pereslete
Tech Booth Crew	Nikki Corso, Ron Gould, Mel Miller, Russell Ham, F. Kaye Porter
Hospitality.	Alta Abbott
Audition Assistants	Gert Nord, Jeanne Spain
Publicity/Photography	Shari Barrett
Postcard/Program Design	Liz Reinhardt
Graphics/Logo Illustration	Justin "Squigs" Robertson
Lobby Artwork	Michael Cohen

CHARACTERS

TED CONNORS – late 20's; young Gary Cooper/Jimmy Stewart type

MORTY KLEIN – early 30's; young Lou Costello/Frank McHugh type

SALLY DUNBAR – late 20's; young Jean Arthur/Barbara Stanwyck type

IDA ROTHBERG – early 30's; young Nancy Walker/Martha Raye type

MRS. KOLOTSKY – early 50's; Ruth Donnelly/Shelley Winters type

CARL BENNETT – mid-teens; young Donald O'Connor/Bobby Van type

SPARKY SCHULTZ – mid-teens; young Mickey Rooney/Frankie Darro type

JOAN McDOOGLE – mid-teens; young Debbie Reynolds/Jane Powell type

NANCY GRIBBLE – mid-teens; young Jane Withers/Judy Garland type

JOEY DeLUCA – pre-teen; cute Scotty Beckett type

GEORGIE JOHNSON – pre-teen; precocious Spanky MacFarland type

MARY GALE – pre-teen; cute Margaret O'Brien type

SUSIE SLAUSON – pre-teen; precocious Natalie Wood type

SETTING

Camp Gitchiegoomie, a wilderness youth retreat in
Northern New Jersey

TIME

Sunday evening; October 30, 1938

AUTHOR'S NOTES

This is intended to be a nostalgic, family-friendly musical, as if conceived and directed by Frank Capra with a score by Rodgers and Hart.

The animal puppets that appear at the doors and windows are optional to the story, but the audience had great fun seeing where they would pop up unexpectedly during the show, for example, at the campsite during the "Boogey Man" song or attacking Morty during the "Little Green Men" song. We used squirrels and raccoons, but other critters can be used at your discretion. Finding ways to hide the puppeteers should be considered when designing your set. But don't let the puppets upstage the actors. Keep their appearances brief and occasional. We found the most realistic-looking puppets at: www.folkmanis.com.

The Goblin costume is something that Mrs. K. supposedly made herself, so it can appear somewhat fake; scary enough to spook the frightened characters on stage, but not so as to terrify young children in the audience. We used a hand-made, over-the-head papier mache globe painted to look like some yeti-creature and a hairy full-length body suit with latex hands and feet. For the actress' comfort, include large eye and nose/mouth holes in the headpiece and a strong zipper or velcro on the back of the body suit for easy access.

During the "No More" song, the purpose of the multi-costumed dancing characters is to confuse Mrs. K. into thinking that something weird is going on. She's not sure whether she's really seeing these things or getting drunk from the wine. It makes her appear more confused and susceptible to believe that Ted, Sally, Morty and Ida's voices are coming from the radio during their prank broadcast. She gets so drunk and panicked that when the "Martians" finally enter, she believes they are real.

The scene change between ACT I, Scenes 3 and 4 can be done fluidly without stopping the action. Have Mrs. K. move downstage as she begins her song, then close the forest curtain. Quietly strike the wall plug, picnic table, barrels, crates, shelves, window curtains and wall dressing and store them off-stage. Pivot units "A" and "B" into place, then set the beds/cots, window curtains, wall dressing and personal props for the cabins. Move the teens and kids into place and open the forest curtain after the audience applauds for Mrs. K.'s song.

We used three different areas of light to separate the interiors of the two cabins and the path between them, keeping the boys on one side, the girls on the other and Ted and Sally on the path (except when they look at their initials carved onto one of the downstage trees). However, for the Busby Berkeley-like dance sequence during the song "Say Goodnight," special lighting combined all three areas into one so people could dance the full width of the stage. Our fantasy tech effects included bubbles, glitter and confetti falling slowly from above. The break at bar 114 in the piano score can be an extended group tap dance sequence (without tap shoes) with percussion accompaniment; e.g. the "Lullaby of Broadway" tap specialty in "42nd Street."

MUSICAL NUMBERS

ACT I:

#1: HALLOWEEN . . . . All (except Sally)

#2: GIRLS AND BOYS . . . . Teens & Kids

#3: HOW THE HECK ARE YA? . . . . Ted & Sally

#4: BOOGEYMAN . . . . Ida, Teens & Kids

#5: I WANNA GET MARRIED . . . . Carl & Joan

#6: WHAT'S AN OLD GYPSY TO DO? . . . . Mrs. Kolotsky

#7: SAY GOODNIGHT . . . . Ida, Morty, Teens & Kids

#8: AND IT ALWAYS MADE YOU SMILE . . . . Ted & Sally

#8A: FINALE – ACT I . . . . All

ACT II:

#9: LITTLE GREEN MEN . . . . All

#10: I WILL BE YOUR HERO . . . . Ida & Morty

#11: FOR EVERY GIRL THERE'S ONE GUY . . . . Joan, Mary & Susie

#12: NO MORE . . . . Mrs. Kolotsky, Ted, Sally, Ida, Morty

#13: FINALE – ACT II . . . . All

ACT ONE

Scene One

(The Dining Hall; sunset; a large open room built like a log cabin with animal heads, Native American blankets, and hand-made rustic crafts hanging on the walls. A few windows reveal the wooded countryside. A main entrance to the outdoors is on one side, with a food service area and a door to the kitchen on the opposite wall. A picnic table is at the center area. Several strands of black and orange paper streamers, a few carved pumpkins and various hand-made Halloween decorations have been placed around the room especially for tonight. A radio is on a table in a downstage corner.)

(The **TEENS** *[*CARL, **SPARKY, JOAN,** *and* **NANCY***] and the* **KIDS** *[*JOEY, **GEORGIE, MARY,** *and* **SUSIE***] are seated at the table, dressed in various hand-made or improvised Halloween costumes, eating dinner.)*

(NOTE: the costumes and make-up should minimally suggest the Halloween characters so as not to distract from their real characters during the first three scenes.)

*(*TED *and* IDA *wear rustic-colored camp counselor uniforms, but* **TED** *also wears a flat-top Frankenstein head and old suit coat, and* **IDA** *wears a "Bride of Frankenstein" wig and a white robe.)*

#1: HALLOWEEN

(The stage is dark. After a short musical introduction, a spotlight comes up on **TED**, *downstage, singing to the audience.)*

TED.

> AT THE END OF OCTOBER,
> ON WHAT THEY CALL "ALL HALLOW'S EVE,"
> ALL THE SPIRITS OF THE UNDERWORLD
> COME OUT TO PLAY, THEY SAY.
>
> *(IDA enters the spotlight.)*

IDA.

> WELL, IT'S THE END OF OCTOBER,
> AND SO WHATEVER YOU BELIEVE,

TED & IDA.

> IF YOU WANT TO SEE SOME SPOOKY THINGS,
> I BET YOU MIGHT TONIGHT.
>
> *(The stage lights come up full, revealing all of the* **TEENS & KIDS** *in the dining hall.)*

TEENS & KIDS.

> OUR FAV'RITE TIME O' YEAR FINALLY IS HERE.
> OH, BOY, OH, BOY, WE REALLY ENJOY HALLOWEEN.
> THAT CREEPY HOLIDAY IS ONE MORE NIGHT AWAY.
> OH, BOY, OH, BOY, WE ALWAYS ENJOY HALLOWEEN.

TEENS.

> WE KNOCK, KNOCK ON EV'RY DOOR
> AND OPEN OUR SACKS

JOEY & GEORGIE.

> FOR LEMON DROPS AND LOLLIPOPS

MARY & SUSIE.

> AND BOXES OF CRACKER JACKS.

TEENS & KIDS.

> HEY, HEY!
> HAVIN' LOTS OF FUN SCARIN' EVERYONE.
> WITCHES AND RATS AND VAMPIRE BATS APPEAR.
> GOBLINS AND GHOULS AND MONSTERS THAT DROOL ARE
>   HERE.
> YEAR IN, YEAR OUT, WE'RE CRAZY ABOUT HALLOWEEN.
>
> *(Dance break, during which* **TED** *and* **IDA** *remove their scary disguises.)*

TEENS & KIDS.

WE RING, RING ON EV'RY DOORBELL,
READY TO YELL:

KIDS.

"TRICK OR TREAT! TRICK OR TREAT!"

TEENS.

FOR CHOC'LATE AND CARAMEL.

TEENS & KIDS.

HEY, HEY,
WHEN THE MOON IS BRIGHT LATE TOMORROW NIGHT,

(short dance break)

YEAR IN, YEAR OUT, WE'RE CRAZY ABOUT HALLOWEEN.

*(As the music underscores, **MRS. KOLOTSKY** enters from the kitchen, wearing a head scarf, shawl and some jewelry like a gypsy fortune teller. She places a large, decorated cake on the picnic table. All of the **TEENS & KIDS** cheer and lunge at the cake.)*

TED & IDA.

EV'ERYBODY EATS FAR TOO MANY SWEETS,
BUT, OH, BOY, OH, BOY, THEY REALLY ENJOY HALLOWEEN.

*(**MORTY** enters from outside. He wears a short-order cook's hat and apron, smeared with dirt and grease.)*

MRS. K.

CANDY BARS AND CAKES GIVE 'EM BELLYACHES,
BUT, OH, BOY, OH, BOY, THEY ALWAYS ENJOY HALLOWEEN.

MORTY. Hey!

IT'S HALF PAST AND GETTIN' LATE.
THE SUN'S GONNA SET.
HAVE THEY PLAYED A GAME? WHAT A SHAME
NOBODY'S BOBBIN' FOR APPLES YET!

(exits into kitchen)

(Music underscores.)

TED. Everybody! Morty's right! The party is almost over –

IDA. – and we haven't played any games!

*(**TEENS & KIDS** cheer loudly.)*

MRS. K. You better hurry, Mr. Connors. That bus has to leave tonight on time!

TED. Alright, here we go, Campers! Line up!

(As the **TEENS & KIDS** *form a line,* **MORTY** *returns from the kitchen with a large metal bucket filled with water and apples.* **TED**, **MORTY** *and* **IDA** *take turns dunking the* **TEENS' & KIDS'** *heads into the bucket, and they come up for air with their faces wet and big red apples stuck in their mouths. They try to sing, then spit the apples back into the bucket.)*

ALL.

HEY, HEY,
WHEN THE MOON IS BRIGHT LATE TOMORROW NIGHT,

TED, IDA, MORTY & MRS. K.

RAGGEDY ANNS AND RAGGEDY ANDYS MEET
MINNIE AND MICKEY MOUSES FOR TRICK OR TREAT.

TEENS & KIDS.

WE GET IN LATE AND PARENTS MIGHT HATE IT
BUT WE WAIT AND WAIT AND ANTICIPATE IT.

ALL.

ALL YEAR IN AND YEAR OUT WE ARE SO CRAZY –
ABOUT HALLOWEEN –

(After the applause, **MRS. K.** *removes her gypsy disguise as* **TED** *stands at the head of the table, banging a cup to quiet the room.* **MORTY** *returns the bucket to the kitchen.)*

TED. Alright, alright. Settle down. We had lots of fun this weekend, but we've run out of food so it's time to get you down the hill and back to civilization.

(Rowdy ad-lib "awwww" from the **TEENS & KIDS** *as they sit at the table.* **MORTY** *re-enters from the kitchen.)*

That is, if Morty can get that old bus running.

MORTY. I don't know, Ted. It was chugging along fine yesterday.

MRS. K. Mr. Klein! It's Sunday evening! We have a responsibility to return these children to their homes and families.

MORTY. I hear ya, Mrs. K., but that ol' junk heap just don't wanna co-operate.

IDA. Is the gas tank full?

MORTY. Yeah, and I checked every hose and thingamajig in the engine and I still can't get it to turn over.

MRS. K. And you call yourself a mechanic!

MORTY. *YOU* call me a mechanic. *AND* a handyman. *AND* a cook. I call myself a slap-happy comedian between jobs in the middle of nowhere!

IDA. Try again, Morty. The kids have school in the morning.

GEORGIE. And Halloween!

(The **TEENS & KIDS** *ad-lib excitedly.)*

MORTY. We could coast down the mountain in neutral. The brakes won't burn out for at least a mile and then we'd be free-wheelin' straight to the bottom.

(The **TEENS & KIDS** *shout and applaud for that idea, but* **MRS. K.** *gives them and* **MORTY** *a silencing look.)*

MRS. K. Children, you've had your party, and your nature weekend here at Camp Gitchiegoomie is coming to an inevitable conclusion.

(The **TEENS & KIDS** *ad-lib "awww.")*

CARL. Can we come back again sometime, Mrs. K.?

MRS. K. Well, Carl, that's up to your parents and the generous Board of Directors who paid for your wilderness adventure. We'll see about that next season.

IDA. If there *IS* a next season.

MRS. K. None of that kind of talk, Miss Rothberg. The reputation of our beloved Camp Gitchiegoomie is as stable as it's always been.

SUSIE. Except for the Goblin!

(The **KIDS** *huddle together, teasing each other, pretending to be scared.* **MORTY** *chuckles and sits on a crate.)*

TED. There is NO Goblin. I've told you a dozen times, there is no scary monster roaming around in the forest up here. Save that for the campfire!

IDA. Honest, kids, it's just some nasty rumor that's been going around.

JOAN. It's the Gitchiegoomie Goblin that's been "goin' around!" We heard him!

SPARKY. Heavy footsteps stumbling in the dark –

GEORGIE. Moaning and groaning real spooky-like –

NANCY. Then howling at the moon like some kind of horrible creature!

MARY. We all heard it!

IDA. *(playfully)* Ohh, that was just Morty in the latrine after last night's Chili Surprise!

*(***MORTY*** reacts, stands.)*

MRS. K. You're scaring yourselves for no reason. Goblin or not, you're all safe and sound for now, and you'll be back in your own beds tonight – hopefully.

*(glares at ***MORTY***)*

CARL. If it's any help, ma'am, me and Sparky know about car engines.

SPARKY. Tops in our auto repair class at school.

MRS. K. *(hedging for an excuse)* Thank you, boys, but my liability insurance won't allow for something like that. Heaven forbid, something should happen to you, I don't know what I'd do.

JOAN. *(sweetly, to* ***CARL****)* Neither do I.

(The ***TEENS & KIDS*** *ad-lib, teasing them.* ***CARL****, embarrassed, moves further away from* ***JOAN****.)*

MRS. K. Mr. Klein, I suggest you return to the "junk heap" and get that thing running before the moon comes up. You know how treacherous that road is at night.

MORTY. *(in a W.C. Fields voice)* 'Tis not a fit night out for Man nor Beast!

(No one is impressed by his imitation. They stare at him silently. **IDA** *punches his arm, and* **MORTY** *exits outside.)*

MRS. K. *(to* **TED** *and* **IDA***)* And the two of you, into my office. We may have a situation here –

(quietly to them)

– and I don't want to discuss it in front of the children.

TED & IDA. Huh?

MRS. K. *(quietly)* I don't want to discuss it in front of the children.

TED & IDA. Eh?

MRS. K. *(loudly)* I don't want to discuss it in front of the children!!

IDA. *(to the* **KIDS & TEENS***)* We'll be right back. Clear off your tables – quietly. Joanie, you're in charge.

JOAN. Yes, ma'am.

*(***MRS. K.***,* **TED** *and* **IDA** *exit into the kitchen. The* **TEENS & KIDS** *take their dinnerware and trash to the food service area.)*

JOEY. Ooooo, Joanie's in charge!

MARY. Better than you, Joey DeLuca!

SUSIE. Yeah, better than you.

SPARKY. Ohh, Joanie's so smart, Joanie's so good, Joanie thinks she knows everything.

JOAN. Well, I do, Schultz. At least more than any city boy.

CARL. I wouldn't bet on that, country girl. You learn an awful lot growin' up on the streets.

NANCY. Yeah, but knowing important stuff; things that matter. That's what we mean.

GEORGIE. Like what?

JOAN. You wouldn't understand. You're boys!

CARL & SPARKY. So?

#2: *GIRLS AND BOYS*

JOAN.

    TO BE A BULLY, AGGRESSIVE AND CRUEL,
    AND MAKE EXCUSES TO GET OUT OF SCHOOL;

JOAN & NANCY.

    THAT'S WHAT LITTLE BOYS WERE MADE FOR,
    AND THAT'S WHY I'M GLAD I'M A GIRL.

NANCY.

    TO BE CONCEITED, ANNOYING AND MEAN,
    AND NEVER KNOW HOW IT FEELS TO BE CLEAN;

JOAN & NANCY.

    THAT'S WHAT LITTLE BOYS WERE MADE FOR,
    AND THAT'S WHY I'M GLAD I'M A GIRL.

CARL & SPARKY.

    BOYS WANT CHOICES, BOYS WANT FREEDOM.

JOAN.

    BOYS WANT GIRLS TO COOK AND FEED 'EM.

NANCY.

    GIRLS WANT BOYS, BUT SURE DON'T NEED 'EM

JOAN & NANCY.

    ESPECIALLY WHEN THEY TRY TO GET FRESH.

MARY & SUSIE. You said it!

(wipe their mouths as if the boys tried to kiss them)

JOAN.

    TO SAY WE'RE CHARMING, ATTRACTIVE AND SWEET,

NANCY.

    THEN SAY IT TO EVERY GIRL THAT YOU MEET!

JOAN & NANCY.

    THAT'S WHAT LITTLE BOYS WERE MADE FOR,
    AND THAT'S WHY I'M GLAD I'M NOT LIKE MY DAD.
    THAT'S WHY I'M GLAD I'M A GIRL.

SPARKY. Ohh, them's fightin' words!

NANCY. You WOULD fight with a girl.

SPARKY. How else can we prove you wrong? You never shut
up long enough to listen to the facts!

JOAN. What facts?

CARL. It's human nature, Joanie. You can't argue with human nature.

TO HAVE THE BABIES AND CLEAN UP THE HOUSE,
TO BE A QUIET, OBEDIENT SPOUSE;

CARL & SPARKY.

THAT'S WHAT LITTLE GIRLS WERE MADE FOR,
AND THAT'S WHY I'M GLAD I'M A BOY.

SPARKY.

TO SEW THE BUTTONS AND WASH ALL THE CLOTHES,
WEAR LOTS OF LIPSTICK AND POWDER YOUR NOSE.

CARL & SPARKY.

THAT'S WHAT LITTLE GIRLS WERE MADE FOR,
AND THAT'S WHY I'M GLAD I'M A BOY.

JOAN & NANCY.

GIRLS LIKE PRESENTS, GIRLS LIKE FLOWERS.

CARL.

GIRLS LIKE BOYS TO SIT FOR HOURS.

SPARKY.

BOYS LIKE GIRLS WITH PEP LIKE OURS

CARL & SPARKY.

UNTIL THEY START TO OPEN THEIR MOUTHS.

JOEY & GEORGIE. Blah, blah, blah!

(wink and shake hands)

CARL.

TO SMILE PRETTY AND BE A GOOD WIFE

SPARKY.

AND NOT WANT ANYTHING MORE OUT OF LIFE;

CARL & SPARKY.

THAT'S WHAT LITTLE GIRLS WERE MADE FOR,
AND THAT'S WHY I'M GLAD I'M JUST LIKE MY DAD.
THAT'S WHY I'M GLAD I'M A BOY.

*(Dance sequence between the **TEENS**; an "any-step-you-can-do-I-can-do-better" contest; then the **KIDS** take over.)*

MARY.

COLLECTING BULL FROGS AND BEETLES AND WORMS,

SUSIE.

AND ANY CREATURE THAT SLITHERS OR SQUIRMS;

MARY & SUSIE.

THAT'S WHAT LITTLE BOYS WERE MADE FOR,
AND THAT'S WHY I'M GLAD I'M A GIRL.

JOEY.

LIKE SHIRLEY TEMPLE, YOU WHINE AND YOU CRY

GEORGIE.

TO GET THE TOYS YOU WANT PARENTS TO BUY;

JOEY & GEORGIE.

THAT'S WHAT LITTLE GIRLS WERE MADE FOR,
AND THAT'S WHY I'M GLAD I'M A BOY.

ALL GIRLS.

GIRLS WANT FAMILIES,

ALL BOYS.

BOYS WANT KISSES,

JOAN & NANCY.

ONLY IF YOU MAKE US MISSES.

CARL & SPARKY.

OUR IDEA OF WEDDED BLISS IS:

JOEY & GEORGIE. *(imitating their fathers)* "I'm goin' out ta-night wid da boys. Don't wait up!"

MARY & SUSIE. *(imitating their mothers)* "Wahhhhh –"

ALL.

WE'D BE SO HAPPY IF YEAR AFTER YEAR
THERE'D BE SOME WAY TO MAKE YOU DISAPPEAR.

GIRLS.	BOYS.
THAT'S WHAT LITTLE GIRLS WERE MADE FOR,	THAT'S WHAT LITTLE BOYS WERE MADE FOR,
AND THAT'S WHY I'M GLAD,	OH, YEAH?
YOU MAKE ME SO MAD!	TOO BAD!
THAT'S WHY I'M GLAD	THAT'S WHY I'M GLAD
I'M A GIRL,	I'M A BOY,
A GIRL, A GIRL, A GIRL –.	A BOY, A BOY, A BOY –.

(After the applause, **TED,** **IDA** *and* **MRS. K.** *enter from the kitchen.)*

MRS. K. Campers! Campers, give me your attention.

(The **TEENS & KIDS** *sit at the table.)*

As you know, there's been a slight delay getting the bus ready for your trip home. I have every confidence that the repairs will be made post haste – but until then –

(There's a loud crash from outside and a car wheel rolls in through the front door. **MORTY** *enters, picks it up, smiles meekly, and exits.* **MRS. K.** *holds up a large tin canister.)*

– but until then, I found one last tin of marshmallows in the pantry so you can all go out to the campfire and –

(The **TEENS & KIDS** *cheer and exit outside with* **IDA** *and the tin.)*

TED. Well, that oughta keep 'em busy for a few minutes.

(sweeps floor with a broom)

MRS. K. What a way to end the season! Everything was going so well this year until now.

(wiping the picnic table with a cloth)

TED. I thought attendance was down, especially there in late August. That's usually our busiest time and half of the cabins were empty.

MRS. K. Well, yes, perhaps in numbers, but in the quality of care and safety, we're still very much on track.

TED. Except for Billy Johnson wandering onto the archery range.

MRS. K. A near miss. The Board of Directors were worried about that one. Luckily, his family is too poor to sue.

*(***TED** *opens the door to sweep out the dirt and chases away an annoying squirrel.)*

TED. Maybe some of the regulars are taking that gossip seriously. Those rumors about "The Goblin" have been circulating for over a year now.

MRS. K. How can people believe such rubbish?

TED. A lot of people swear they've seen The Jersey Devil.

MRS. K. To promote tourism in those small towns around the Pinelands. It's a boon to their economy. A child-eating monster prowling up here only discourages parents from sending me their children.

TED. Not good news for the Board either; probably K.O.'s the property value.

(exits into the kitchen with the rest of the Halloween cake)

MRS. K. *(mysteriously, to herself)* Yes – it does.

(The **TEENS & KIDS** *scream from offstage.)*

SALLY. *(off)* Sorry! Oh, I'm so sorry.

MRS. K. Now who's that?

*(**SALLY DUNBAR** enters; an attractive young woman, obviously from the big city by the way she dresses and talks.)*

MRS. K. Who are you? What are you doing up here this time of night? What do you want?

SALLY. One at a time. I'm still a little out of breath. Sally Dunbar. New York Tribune. How are ya? There was nobody to meet me down below so I hitched a ride partway on a hay wagon with a – Mr. Hutchins? Hootchins?

MRS. K. Hootkins. He has a farm a couple miles from the main road.

SALLY. Well, lucky for me. Are you Elaine Kolotsky?

MRS. K. I am.

SALLY. We spoke on the phone last week; about me doing a story on Camp Gitchiegoomie? Closing weekend? Maybe closing for good?

MRS. K. *(more excuses)* Oh, my goodness. Yes. I was so busy that day. I completely forgot about it.

SALLY. A good story is a good story and I wasn't gonna let this one get by me. Can I have a glass of something?

MRS. K. Oh, of course.

(shouts towards the kitchen)

Mr. Connors, could you bring out a glass of lemonade?

TED. *(off)* You got it, Mrs. K.

SALLY. Hey, I'm sorry about scarin' the kids out there by the campfire. The old guy dropped me off at the bridge. I had to walk the rest of the way up in these heels. It's almost dark and I guess I stumbled out from the bushes.

MRS. K. Not to worry. The campers love to tell spooky stories this time every night. They're ready to scream at anything, –

(obviously perturbed)

– even a reporter from The Tribune.

*(As **SALLY** brushes off her muddy shoes, **TED** enters from the kitchen with the glass of lemonade. **MRS. K.** points to **SALLY** and **TED** offers her the glass.)*

SALLY. *(to **MRS. K.**)* So what can you tell me about this Gitchiegoomie Goblin?

*(looking up, taking the glass from **TED**)*

Thanks.

TED. Sally? Sally Dunbar?

SALLY. Ted?

(A friendly handshake between them turns into a hesitant, affectionate hug.)

TED. My, gosh! What are you doing back here?

SALLY. How about you? You were going into business with your uncle or something.

TED. Ohh, that never got off the ground. What was that? Ten years ago?

SALLY. Yeah, something like that. I'm a reporter for The Tribune in New York. I'm doing a story on our old stomping ground.

TED. I don't believe it!

MRS. K. You're an alumnus of Camp Gitchiegoomie?

TED. Sally and I were campers here during high school; summer of '26 or '27?

SALLY. We carved our initials on an elm tree out there by the girls' cabins.

TED. Still there, above eye level now.

SALLY. Remember the blue ribbon for the relay race finals?

TED. Did you take that home? It's not on MY wall.

MRS. K. *(seizing the chance to get away)* Well, how lovely for you. There must be so much to catch up on. Why don't you two take a moment to get reacquainted? I'll see what's keeping Mr. Klein and that stubborn jalopy of a bus.

SALLY. But, Mrs. Kolotsky, I really want to ask you –

MRS. K. Please, dear, it's "Mrs. K." to everyone around here. There's more lemonade out back. I'll just be a few minutes.

*(**MRS. K.** opens the door, kicks at the annoying squirrel, and exits outside **TED** and **SALLY** awkwardly size each other up. The **TEENS & KIDS** scream from offstage.)*

MRS. K. *(off)* Sorry!

TED. Sally Dunbar.

SALLY. Ted "Beanstalk" Connors.

#3: HOW THE HECK ARE YA?

TED. Well.

SALLY. Yeah, Well.

TED.

SO HOW THE HECK ARE YA?
HOW LONG HAS IT BEEN?
I HAVE TO CONFESS I GUESS IT'S GOOD YOU'RE HERE
   AGAIN.
IT SEEMS THE YEARS HAVE BEEN KIND.
YOU'RE GROWN UP AND REFINED,
AND YOUR TEETH ARE ALIGNED, TOP AND BOTTOM.

SALLY. And worth every penny!

TED.

> SO HOW THE HECK ARE YA?
> YOU HARDLY HAVE CHANGED
> EXCEPT IN SOME PLACES MOTHER NATURE'S RE-ARRANGED.
> LET'S SHARE A GLASS, HAVE A SHOT,
> AND SEE WHO REMEMBERS WHAT.
> HEY, HOW THE HECK ARE YOU?

SALLY.

> SO HOW THE HECK ARE YA?
> HOW LONG HAS IT BEEN?
> YOU'RE PRACTICALLY JUST AS I RECALL BUT NOT AS THIN.
> YOU HAD A HEAD FULL OF SCHEMES
> AND A HEART FULL OF DREAMS,
> AND, BY GOLLY, IT SEEMS YOU STILL GOT 'EM!

TED. Rome wasn't built in a day!

SALLY.

> SO HOW THE HECK ARE YA?
> WHO NEEDS TO BE RICH
> AS LONG AS YOU GET THROUGH EVERY DAY WITHOUT A
>   HITCH.
> SOMETIMES I CREAK OR I CRACK
> OR I FALL FLAT ON MY BACK,
> BUT HOW THE HECK ARE YOU?

TED.

> CITY LIFE, I S'POSE, CAN BE EXCITING.

SALLY.

> COUNTRY LIFE, FOR SOME, IS WORTH THE FUSS.

TED.

> BUT IT'S A WELL-KNOWN FACT
> THAT OPPOSITES ATTRACT.

SALLY.

> IT'S HARD TO FIND TWO MORE ATTRACTIVE
> OPPOSITES THAN US.

BOTH.

> SO HOW THE HECK ARE YA?
> HOW LONG HAS IT BEEN?

TED.

WE OUGHTA CATCH UP ON THINGS,

SALLY.

BUT WHERE DO WE BEGIN?

TED.

I TOOK A CHANCE,

SALLY.

SO DID I.

TED.

BEAT THE ODDS, BY AND BY.

SALLY.

AND WHEN THINGS WENT AWRY, I FORGOT 'EM.

TED. What else can you do?

SALLY.

SO HOW THE HECK ARE YA?

TED.

I'M DOIN' O.K.

I MAKE IT A POINT EACH DAY TO KICK THE CLOUDS AWAY.

WHILE I WAS HERE,

SALLY.

I WAS THERE.

BOTH.

BUT WE'RE NONE THE WORSE FOR WEAR.

HEY, HOW THE HECK ARE YOU?

(dance sequence, then,)

TED.

WHILE I WAS HERE

SALLY.

I WAS THERE.

BOTH.

BUT WE'RE NONE THE WORSE FOR WEAR.

HEY, HOW THE HECK,

I SAY, HOW THE HECK,

TELL ME, HOW THE HECK ARE YOU – ?

(blackout)

#3-A: SCENE CHANGE

Scene Two

(The Campfire; immediately following; a wooded area near the dining hall; Darkness has arrived; there's moonlight, stars and the sounds of crickets and frogs in the distance. **IDA** *and the* **TEENS & KIDS** *are seated around a glowing campfire made from logs and rocks. Most of them have blankets wrapped around their shoulders and are holding long sticks toasting marshmallows over the fire.* **IDA** *is telling them what she thinks is a spooky story.)*

IDA. And he ran through the house – thump-thump, thump-thump. What was wrong with those stupid policemen? Couldn't they hear it? – thump-thump, thump-thump – And when they ripped open the floorboards next to the bed, they finally found the old man's disgusting, rotting corpse. And that sound – that sound –

TEENS & KIDS. *(bored to death)* "…was the beating of the old man's heart."

IDA. You kids got ice water in your veins?

MARY. That wasn't scary.

SUSIE. Bippy the Clown told that one on the radio last week.

CARL. Ida, we saw that coming a mile away.

NANCY. Thump-thump, thump-thump! Of course, it was his heart.

IDA. But that's a classic. It scares everybody. Did ya hear the one about the guy in this pit with a big pendulum –

TEENS & KIDS. *(ad-lib)* Naw – heard it – that's not scary – no, no –

JOAN. Face it, Ida. People from your time were scared by different kinds of things than we are.

IDA. From MY time? I'm not THAT old!

MARY. Don't you know anything about Dracula or the Werewolf?

SPARKY. Or King Kong? He's my favorite!

*(**SPARKY** and **NANCY** imitate Kong and Ann Darrow. When he tries to put his hand where he shouldn't, she pulls away.)*

NANCY. Don't get any ideas, you big baboon.

IDA. Your parents let you see those kinds of movies?

CARL. They give us a quarter just to get us out of the house on a Saturday afternoon, and off we go.

JOAN. Cartoons, newsreels, coming attractions, a chapter story, and then –

TEENS & KIDS. Monster movies!

#4: BOOGEYMAN

*(**JOEY, GEORGIE, MARY** and **SUSIE** leap up towards **IDA** and growl like monsters. The **TEENS** laugh, and the **KIDS** cross below the campfire.)*

KIDS.

THE BOOGEYMAN IS GONNA GET YOU.
YOU NEVER KNOW WHERE HE WILL BE.
INSIDE THE CLOSET, BENEATH THE STAIRS
OR BEHIND THE VERY NEXT TREE.

TEENS. Watch out!

*(**IDA** nervously plays along.)*

KIDS.

HE'S HIDING SO YOU CANNOT SEE HIM.
NO MATTER WHAT YOU DO, BEWARE!
THE ONE TIME WHEN YOU DON'T EXPECT IT,
THE BOOGEYMAN WILL BE RIGHT THERE.

(short dance break)

JOEY.

FRANKENSTEIN IS BIG AND SCARY.
HE COULD TEAR YOU LIMB FROM LIMB.

MARY.

THE INVISIBLE MAN COULD BE STANDING BESIDE YOU
AND YOU'D NEVER KNOW IT WAS HIM.

GEORGIE.

>ZOMBIES COULD BE AT THE WINDOW.
>MUMMIES COULD BE AT THE DOOR.

SUSIE.

>AND WHO'S THAT CRAWLING UNDERNEATH THE FLOOR?

KIDS.

>THE BOOGEYMAN IS GONNA GET YOU.
>HE'S WAITIN' 'TIL YOU TURN YOUR BACK.
>THE NIGHT IS STILL AND THE MOON IS FULL.
>THAT'S WHEN HE GOES ON THE ATTACK.

TEENS. Watch out!

KIDS.

>YOU BETTER KEEP YOUR EYES WIDE OPEN.
>'CAUSE IF YOU WALK ALONE SOMEWHERE,
>THE ONE TIME WHEN YOU DON'T EXPECT IT,
>THE BOOGEYMAN WILL BE RIGHT THERE.

>*(Dance sequence, the* **KIDS** *imitate monsters and scare* **IDA***; then:)*

TEENS & KIDS.

>THE BOOGEYMAN IS GONNA GET YOU.
>YOU ALWAYS GOTTA BE ON GUARD,
>AND CAREFUL RUNNING ON BUSY STREETS
>OR IN ANYBODY'S BACKYARD.

>*(A deep booming voice from the forest says "Watch out!" and* **IDA** *screams.)*

>HE'S PLAYING HIDE AND SEEK AROUND YOU,
>AND NEVER PLAYS IT FAIR AND SQUARE.
>THE ONE TIME WHEN YOU DON'T EXPECT IT –

>*(They stalk* **IDA** *from one direction.)*

>YOU LOOK AWAY AND DON'T SUSPECT IT –

>*(They stalk her from the other direction.)*

>THE BOOGEYMAN WILL BE – RIGHT – THERE –

>*(The* **TEENS & KIDS** *point one way,* **IDA** *trembles.)*

>THERE!

>*(same business, opposite side)*

TEENS & KIDS. *(cont.)*

THERE!

(Same business, and **IDA** *hides under a blanket. As the* **TEENS & KIDS** *laugh, a gust of wind makes the campfire roar and large scary shadows dance across the trees. Everyone hides under their blankets.)*

(blackout)

#4-A: SCENE CHANGE

Scene Three

(The Dining Hall; immediately following; **TED** *and* **SALLY** *are seated at the picnic table, sipping their glasses of lemonade, laughing about old times.)*

SALLY. No, no. I put the firecracker in the tomato soup. You thought of it, but I was the only camper that summer with the nerve to actually do it.

TED. But Mr. Hausenmeyer caught *me* running away and I was the one scraping it off the walls all weekend.

*(***MRS. K.*** cautiously pokes her head in through the kitchen door.)*

SALLY. Hey there, Mrs. K.

MRS. K. *(caught, she enters)* Sounds like you two are having a wonderful time. How nice. Mr. Connors, it's nearly eight o'clock. We have to make a decision.

TED. We don't have much choice, Mrs. K. We'll keep the kids overnight and telephone their parents so they can pick them up first thing in the morning.

SALLY. Is there some problem?

MRS. K. We have a broken-down camp bus and a handy-man who isn't all that handy. The mountain road is too narrow and treacherous for anyone to drive up at night –

TED. Or walk it. I don't know how you made it.

SALLY. Tenacity, my friend. When I set out to do something, I never give up. A good reporter learns that the hard way.

TED. *(re: her muddy high heels)* Well, good reporter, you won't be going far in THOSE shoes. There must be a pair of moccasins around here somewhere.

(looks in cabinet)

(As **SALLY** *bends over to remove her shoes, the* **TEENS & KIDS** *scream from offstage.* **MORTY** *enters from outside, more disheveled than ever, carrying the tailpipe from the bus.)*

MORTY. *(to the* **TEENS & KIDS***)* Sorry!

IDA. *(off)* Morty, you blockhead! You scared the livin' you-know-what outta me!

MORTY. Well, what are you doing under that blanket?

(accidentally gooses **SALLY** *with the tailpipe)*

Oh. 'Scuse me.

(closes the door)

TED. Morty, this is Sally Dunbar; reporter from The New York Tribune, former camper, and a very old personal friend.

SALLY. You're the handyman?

MORTY. Only when the WPA is looking. Otherwise, it's Morty Klein, jokes, impressions and snappy patter for every occasion.

SALLY. 'Spleasure.

(shakes Morty's greasy hand; reacts)

MRS. K. And what's the word on the bus, Mr. Klein?

MORTY. Broken; "broken" is the word for that old beer wagon.

TED. Then we might as well get the kids to bed.

SALLY. So you're saying we're stuck out here until morning?

*(***SUSIE*** *enters quietly from the kitchen, crosses behind them to the radio at the corner table.)*

MORTY. No guardrails on that road and a sheer drop on several curves. I wouldn't risk walking the kids down, OR having their parents drive up at night.

SALLY. What about this Mr. Hootchins and his hay wagon?

MRS. K. Mr. *Hootkins* has no telephone, my dear. No, we'd better bunk down for the night and send them off in the morning.

MORTY. Heck of a time for the bus to konk out on us –

(in a Boris Karloff voice)

– especially with that monster roaming around out there.

(**SUSIE** *turns on the radio and the static and music startles everyone.*)

TED. Susie! Gosh, what are you doing in here?

SUSIE. Sunday night; time for my program.

MRS. K. Little girl, you should be out with the others at the campfire.

SUSIE. Too scary. I never miss Charlie on Sunday nights.

MRS. K. Turn that thing off and come outside with us. I have an announcement to make.

(**SUSIE** *turns the radio off and crosses next to* **MRS. K.**)

SALLY. Mrs. Kolotsky, I came all the way up here for an interview. I skinned both elbows and ruined a five dollar pair of shoes. If you could just answer a couple questions, I can phone the story into my editor and make the morning edition.

MRS. K. Miss Dunbar, I'm responsible for the safety of those innocent children out there. They should have been returned to the loving arms of their families over an hour ago. I'll bed them down in their cabins, telephone their parents, *then* perhaps we can talk about – whatever it is you have on your mind.

(**MRS. K.** *'s gentle embrace on* **SUSIE** *has turned into a choke-hold around her neck, and* **TED** *releases the gasping girl. Flustered,* **MRS. K.** *glares at* **MORTY.**)

This is all *your* fault.

MORTY. *(in a Jack Benny voice)* Well!

MRS. K. *(calling offstage)* We're coming out! It's only us. Don't be alarmed!

(**MRS. K.** *exits outside, followed by* **MORTY.** **TED** *and* **SALLY** *exchange an amused look then follow with* **SUSIE.** **TED** *flips a light switch off and moonlight comes in through the windows. After a beat,* **CARL** *and* **JOAN** *enter playfully from the kitchen.*)

CARL. Will you stop that! We're going to get in trouble.

JOAN. What can they do? Send us home??

(tickles him)

CARL. Cut it out. I never should've told you where I'm ticklish.

JOAN. Uh-hmm!

CARL. And I don't know where *you're* ticklish.

JOAN. For me to know and you to find out!

CARL. Shh! They can hear you.

JOAN. Oh, they can not!

CARL. Can, too! Sparky knows my pals at school. He could tell them all about this.

JOAN. About what? That you have — a girlfriend??

CARL. No, no. You're a girl, and you're a friend, but none of this "girlfriend" stuff. I have a reputation to think of.

JOAN. Reputation as a what?

*(**SUSIE** enters from the kitchen in the dark and crosses to the radio.)*

CARL. Listen, Joan. I like you — a lot. I don't understand why. I just do. You make me wanna put down my books and comb my hair and skip meals.

JOAN. Well, I guess that's a compliment.

CARL. You get me all confused. Two more years and my father's pulling some strings to get me into college. I can't let him down. I don't have time for this love stuff.

JOAN. Love stuff? You make it sound like a disease.

*(**SUSIE** turns on the radio and startles them with sudden music. **CARL** turns the lights on.)*

CARL. Susie, you're supposed to be out by the campfire.

SUSIE. So are you.

JOAN. We — have business to discuss.

SUSIE. Kissy smoochy business. It's almost time for Charlie.

JOAN. It's not kissy smoochy business. It's just — talk. We're just talking.

CARL. And you better not tell anyone what we were talking about!

(SUSIE *puckers her lips and makes "kissy" sounds at them, then turns the dial on the radio to another station.*)

JOAN. Susie Slauson, I'm your cabin leader. You turn off that radio and get out of here.

SUSIE. Uh-uh, Joanie. That only works when we're *in* the cabin. Ida says.

CARL. That's it. The kid's got us. We're busted by a six-year-old.

SUSIE. I'm seven.

CARL. You wanna be eight?

SUSIE. You wanna cut the chatter? I can't find my program.

JOAN. Susie, please – as a favor to me – for all the extra cookies I let you sneak at dinner –

CARL. And all the times I led your pony around the track?

SUSIE. *(turns off the radio)* Well, alright. But make it snappy. I never miss Charlie on Sunday night.

(imitating Charlie)

Kiss her and get it over with or "I'll mow ya down!"

(hits the light switch, leaving only moonlight again, and exits outside.)

JOAN. Kids; you gotta love 'em.

CARL. Why?

JOAN. And someday, Carl, we'll have a whole bunch of our own.

CARL. Whoa!! Hold on a minute there, lady! Did we just skip ahead a few chapters?

JOAN. Isn't that what we're talking about? You like-a me and I like-a you –

CARL. Yeah, sure. But how did we get a whole nursery of our own all of a sudden?

JOAN. Silly boy. Don't you know anything about this "love stuff?"

#5: I WANNA GET MARRIED

JOAN. *(cont.)*

> OH, I WANNA GET MARRIED SOMEDAY.
> I WANNA BE SOMEONE'S BRIDE.
> TAKIN' A VOW WITH THE BOY OF MY DREAMS
> STANDIN' THERE BY MY SIDE.
>
> I WANNA SEE FATHER BEAMING.
> I WANNA SEE MOTHER CRY.
> MOST OF ALL I WANT THE WORLD TO KNOW
> I LOVE A WONDERFUL GUY.
>
>> HEAR HOW THE WEDDING BELLS
>> ARE DINGING AND DONGING FOR ME.
>> SEE ALL MY FRIENDS AND FAMILY

CARL.

>> EATING AND DRINKING FOR FREE.

JOAN.

>> YES, I WANNA WEAR SOMETHING BORROWED.
>> I WANNA WEAR SOMETHING BLUE.
>> BUT THE MOST IMPORTANT THING THAT I WANT
>> TO MAKE SURE IT ALL COMES TRUE,
>> I WANNA MAKE SURE I MARRY YOU.

(Dance break, then JOAN *freezes as gloomy lights focus on* CARL.*)*

CARL.

>> WHY DO I FEEL LIKE A PRIS'NER IN THIS ROOM?
>> WHY DO I FEEL AN IMPENDING SENSE OF DOOM?

*(*GEORGIE, SUSIE, JOEY *and* MARY, *dressed as brides and grooms, enter and criss-cross in front of* CARL, *the brides holding leashes that are wrapped around the grooms' wrists.)*

>> HOLY MATRIMONY IS SO MUCH BALONEY
>> WHEN YOU'RE A YOUNG AND AMBITIOUS GUY LIKE ME.

(The gloomy lights disappear as the two couples exit.)

> I DON'T WANNA GET MARRIED SOMEDAY.
> I DON'T WANNA BE SOMEONE'S GROOM.

CARL. *(cont.)*

SEEIN' THE BIG PLANS I MADE FOR MYSELF
SUDDENLY GO KABOOM.

I DON'T WANNA WALK DOWN THE AISLE.
I DON'T WANNA GET HIT WITH RICE.
ANYONE WHO THINKS THAT'S SOME KIND OF FUN
SHOULD GET PSYCHIATRIC ADVICE.

HEAR HOW THE WEDDING BELLS
ARE TOLLING DISASTER FOR ME.
SEE HOW YOUR FAMILY'S ASKING,
"HOW MANY KIDS WILL THERE BE?"

JOAN. First one, then two, then three –

CARL. Aw, gee!!

JOAN.	**CARL.**
I WANNA GET MARRIED SOMEDAY.	DON'T WANNA GET MARRIED;
I WANNA BE SOMEONE'S BRIDE.	DON'T WANNA NEW BRIDE.
BUT THE MOST IMPORTANT THING THAT I WANT TO MAKE SURE IT ALL COMES TRUE,	BUT THE MOST IMPORTANT THING THAT I WANT TO MAKE SURE IT ALL COMES TRUE,
I WANNA MAKE SURE I –	
	I WANNA MAKE SURE YOU DON'T,
WANNA MAKE YOU SAY "I DO,"	
	I NEVER WILL SAY IT!
I WANNA MAKE SURE I MARRY YOU –	I WANNA MAKE SURE I DON'T MARRY YOU –.

*(After the applause, **MRS. K.** enters from outside and switches on the lights. **CARL** and **JOAN** pretend to be "cleaning" – in the dark! – and nonchalantly avoid **MRS. K.**'s suspicious gaze. **MRS. K.** chases away the squirrels and raccoons that have been watching at the windows, then shouts out through the door.)*

MRS. K. Yes, they're in here.

(All of the others enter from outside and sit at the table. **SUSIE** *hovers near the radio.)*

TED. So that's the situation. We're going to spend one more night here, then your parents will come up and get you in the morning.

(The **TEENS & KIDS** *cheer.)*

MRS. K. But all cabin rules still apply. No rough-housing, no mischief, no leaving the premises –

(a look to **CARL** *and* **JOAN***)*

– and no fraternizing between cabins.

SALLY. *(to* **TED***)* And I thought *our* rules were tough.

GEORGIE. Do we get anything to eat?

TED. Did you finish that whole tin of marshmallows?

MARY. What was left, after the boys got to it first.

JOEY. We shared!

NANCY. The burnt ones!

IDA. If I find anything in the pantry, I'll bring it along. You can take the costumes home with you tomorrow. Tonight, it's jammies and long woolies.

TED. Now let's show Miss Dunbar how we proceed to the cabins for bedtime.

*(***TED*** blows a whistle, the* **TEENS & KIDS** *form a straight line, facing the main door. He blows again, and they turn "right face." Before he blows again, they "cheer" and run out the door.* **IDA** *and* **MORTY** *chase after them and exit.)*

SALLY. Mrs. Kolotsky –

MRS. K. I can offer you a bed in the girls' cabin. All the comforts of home, and then some.

SALLY. Thank you. But if I could just have five minutes of your time –

MRS. K. There's so much to do tonight. Couldn't it wait?

SALLY. I'd really like to make that morning edition. My editor would be so happy to get this story out for Halloween.

(milking the melodrama)

SALLY. *(cont.)* He's not a happy man, the paper's circulation is down, he's facing an early retirement –

*(***TED*** *mimes playing a sad violin, then signals* ***SALLY*** *that he'll meet her outside, and exits.)*

MRS. K. If you must.

(polite, but stalling; sits)

What is it you want to know, Miss Dunbar?

SALLY. These rumors about a Gitchiegoomie Goblin; any idea where they came from?

MRS. K. Goodness, how should I know? People say the strangest things.

SALLY. But attendance has been down here for the past two years.

MRS. K. Well, yes –

SALLY. So even though your Board of Directors continues to sponsor these poor city kids for a few days in the country, parents aren't signing up for fear of their children's safety.

MRS. K. There's no proof of that.

SALLY. Whether or not this goblin creature is real or imaginary –

MRS. K. What do you mean, "whether or not?" No such "monster" could exist in this day and age. Or in ANY day and age, for that matter!

SALLY. I've combed through the records. There've been some pretty reliable sightings of this thing. Big and hairy and green; glowing eyes, huge teeth –

MRS. K. Miss Dunbar, I thought your paper stood for some standard of excellence. Are you writing for the news section or the funny pages?

SALLY. Just trying to get the truth, Mrs. K. My sources tell me that business is so bad, the market value of this land has gone through the basement, and the Board is ready to sell to the first buyer for whatever they can get.

(As **MRS. K.** *moves* **SALLY** *towards the main door,* **SUSIE** *sneaks in behind them from the kitchen, unplugs the radio, and exits with it into the kitchen.)*

MRS. K. Well, your sources had better ask the Board about that. I just run this humble little camp on a day-to-day basis, trying to create joy and memories for all those children less fortunate than ourselves.

SALLY. Weren't you involved in some shady real estate dealings several years ago in Atlantic City?

MRS. K. Shady?

SALLY. Questionable – as in, not quite on the up-and-up?

MRS. K. Your cabin is down there on the right, Miss Dunbar. Pleasant dreams.

SALLY. I *know* where the girls' cabin is. I suspect I know a few other things about ol' Camp Gitchiegoomie as well.

MRS. K. Goodnight.

*(**SALLY** exits through the main door. **MRS. K.** leans against it and sighs.)*

#6: WHAT'S AN OLD GYPSY TO DO?

SHE COULD BE TROUBLE; THEY ALWAYS ARE;
CURIOUS REPORTERS FROM "THE TRIBUNE" OR "THE STAR."
QUIZZING ME WITH QUESTIONS, ACCUSING ME OF CRIMES,
THEN PRINTING ALLEGATIONS IN "THE JOURNAL" OR "THE
    TIMES."

CAN'T THEY BE MORE THOUGHTFUL AND FORGIVING
TO A HELPLESS WIDOW SIMPLY TRYING TO EARN A LIVING?

I'VE DEPENDED ON MEN, AGAIN AND AGAIN,
BUT THEIR PROMISES DON'T COME TRUE.
THEY LEAVE ME AFTER THEY DECEIVE ME.
LIKE SOME OLD GOULASH GONE ROTTEN,
I SIT THERE FORGOTTEN.
WHAT'S AN OLD GYPSY TO DO?

MRS. K. *(cont.)*

> I NEED SHOES ON MY FEET AND SOMETHING TO EAT;
> PAY MY LANDLORD THE SAME AS YOU.
> I OUGHT TO DO THE THINGS I'M TAUGHT TO.
> BUT IN A STATE OF FATIGUE I'LL
> TRY SOMETHING ILLEGAL.
> WHAT'S AN OLD GYPSY TO DO?
>
>> I ADMIT WITHOUT ANY APOLOGY
>> ADVISING CONGRESSMEN WITH ASTROLOGY.
>> NINE YEARS AGO, THE PLANETS ALIGNED.
>> THOSE WHO PAID ME CASH SOLD BEFORE THE CRASH.
>
> I MADE WATERED-DOWN HOOTCH, I DANCED AS A COOTCH,
> AND I HEISTED A BANK OR TWO.
> THEY SHOT ME, BUT THEY NEVER CAUGHT ME.
> I MOVE FROM CITY TO CITY.
> THOSE COPS HAVE NO PITY.
> THAT'S WHAT A GYPSY, BORN IN POUGHKEEPSIE,
> WHAT AN OLD GYPSY MUST DO.
>
> I tried to go legit. I really did! But I had the most awful
> luck whenever I went after the honest dollar.
>
> I BOUGHT TENEMENT SLUMS, EVICTED THE BUMS,
> THEN REPAINTED THEM LIKE BRAND NEW.
> VIBRATIONS UNDER THE FOUNDATIONS
> MADE HEALTH INSPECTORS DETERMINE
> I'D BOUGHT LOTS OF VERMIN.
> WHAT'S AN OLD GYPSY TO DO?
>
> THEN I DESPERATELY TOOK A JOB AS A COOK
> AT A SCHRAFT'S ON FIFTH AVENUE.
> OLD FOGIES CHOKED ON MY PEROGIES.
> MY BLINTZES STAYED ON THE DISHES.
> I KILLED WITH MY KNISHES.
> WHAT'S AN OLD GYPSY TO DO?
>
>> THEN WHEN CAMP GITCHIEGOOMIE HIRED ME
>> AFTER F.W. WOOLWORTH FIRED ME,
>> SUDDENLY I'M IN CHARGE OF ALL THIS!
>> OPPORTUNITY FINALLY KNOCKED FOR ME!

MRS. K. *(cont.)* They're ready to sell this land for pennies on the dollar thanks to MY well-placed rumors about that nasty Goblin. And I'll snatch it up and build my own luxurious Oasis for the Privileged Elite. I think it's time for The Goblin himself to chase these little campers clear off the mountain for good. And what's better than on the night before Halloween! Ha-ha –
I'LL LET THE FULL MOON PREPARE 'EM,
THEN DRESS UP AND SCARE 'EM.
THAT'S WHAT A GYPSY –
WHEN SHE'S NOT TIPSY –
WHAT THIS OLD GYPSY – WILL DO!

(blackout)

#6-A: SCENE CHANGE

Scene Four

(The Cabins; immediately following; This is a split set: the interior of the girls' cabin is on one side, the interior of the boys' cabin is on the other side, and the cabins are separated by a wooded path indicating the exterior between them. Moonlight and stars are seen above. Both cabins are built out of logs and beams, with one side door leading to the exterior and to the counselor's room. Two bunk beds and cots are against the walls with pillows, sheets and blankets. The window curtains and bed sheets are various green colors, to be used later in Act Two. The TEENS & KIDS' suitcases, toys and personal items litter the corners and the floors. SUSIE has plugged in the radio next to her bed.)

(As the lights come up, both sets of TEENS & KIDS are half-dressed, some still in their costumes, some partially in pajamas, and are engaged in raucous pillow fights within their own cabins. After several moments, IDA and MORTY enter from their respective rooms; she in a woolen robe and hair curlers, he wearing baggy red long johns and a bathrobe. They try unsuccessfully to stop the pillow fights by being calm and controlled, then both shout "Quiet!" as loud as they can.)

#7: SAY GOODNIGHT

(The TEENS & KIDS freeze in mid-battle.)

IDA.

PUT DOWN THE PILLOWS AND BLANKETS AND FIND YOUR PAJAMAS.
IT'S TIME TO GET INTO BED AND TO SAY GOODNIGHT.

MORTY.

DON'T WANT ANY TANTRUMS OR TROUBLES OR TRAUMAS OR I'M GONNA TELL ALL YOUR PAPAS AND MAMAS.

IDA & MORTY.

WASH UP YOUR HANDS AND YOUR FACES AND SAY GOODNIGHT.

MORTY.

> NO MORE WRESTLING AND ROARING,
> I WANT TO HEAR SNORING WHEN I TURN OFF THE
> LIGHT.

IDA.

> IF ANYONE EVEN WHISPERS "PILLOW FIGHT,"

IDA & MORTY.

> YOU'LL BE IN DOUBLE TROUBLE.
>
> NO EXPLANATIONS, EXCEPTIONS, EXCUSES.
> I WANT EVERYBODY AGREEING TO TRUCES.
> GO DRINK A BIG GLASS OF WATER
> AND SAY GOODNIGHT.

> *(As the music vamps, the* **TEENS & KIDS** *slowly sit on their beds.* **IDA** *and* **MORTY** *tip-toeing backwards, waving goodnight and holding their finger to their lips, quietly exit back into their rooms. The* **TEENS & KIDS** *suddenly jump up with their pillows and blankets and dance as if they were doing a big Ziegfeld Follies-type number.)*

TEENS & KIDS.

> HIT ME WITH YOUR PILLOW.
> HIT ME ONCE AGAIN.
> TURN AROUND AND GET IN LINE
> AND I'LL HIT YOU WITH MINE.
> HAH!
>
> ISN'T THIS, ISN'T THAT, ISN'T THIS SO MUCH FUN?
> START ALL OVER,
> HIT ME WITH YOUR FLUFFY PILLOW.
> HIT ME ONCE MORE.

> *(A few more dance choruses are filled with extravagant Busby-Berkeley-type effects, kaleidoscopic designs and tap routines.* **IDA** *and* **MORTY** *appear from their rooms and join the campers dancing and singing in counterpoint.)*

IDA & MORTY.

PUT DOWN THE PILLOWS
    AND BLANKETS
AND FIND YOUR PAJAMAS.
IT'S TIME TO GET INTO
    BED
AND TO SAY GOODNIGHT.
DON'T WANT ANY
    TANTRUMS
OR TROUBLES OR
    TRAUMAS,
OR I'M GONNA TELL ALL
    YOUR
PAPAS AND MAMAS.
WASH UP YOUR HANDS AND
    YOUR FACES
AND SAY GOODNIGHT.
NO MORE WRESTLING AND
    ROARING.
I WANT TO HEAR SNORING
WHEN I TURN OFF THE
    LIGHT.

IF ANYONE EVEN WHISPERS,
"PILLOW FIGHT,"

TEENS & KIDS.

HIT ME WITH YOUR
    PILLOW.

HIT ME ONCE

AGAIN.
TURN AROUND

AND GET IN LINE

AND I'LL
HIT YOU

WITH MINE. HAH!
ISN'T THIS,

ISN'T THAT,
ISN'T THIS

SO MUCH FUN?

(The **TEENS & KIDS** *softly start chanting "pillow fight," build in intensity, then finally yell loudly, swinging their pillows at* **IDA** *and* **MORTY**.)

IDA & MORTY.

NO EXPLANATIONS, EXCEPTIONS, EXCUSES.
I WANT EVERYBODY AGREEING TO TRUCES.
I'M COUNTING TO FIVE AND THEN
I'M TURNING OUT THE LIGHT –

(As **IDA** *and* **MORTY** *slowly count to "five," the* **TEENS & KIDS** *quickly rip off their costumes and clothes, revealing their sleepwear underneath, and jump into their beds and snore just as* **IDA** *and* **MORTY** *say "five," hit the light switches – which darken the rooms – and exit into their own rooms.)*

(After the applause, **SUSIE** *turns on the radio and we see the light shining under her blanket and hear several seconds of an Edgar Bergen and Charlie McCarthy radio show broadcast.* **IDA** *quickly pokes her head into the room with a lit flashlight and the radio goes off. After a silent beat, she exits into her room. The radio goes on again and we hear Edgar bantering with Charlie.* **IDA** *quickly pokes her head into the room again and the radio goes off. After a silent beat, she exits into her room. After a few more silent beats, someone farts loudly in the boys' cabin.* **MORTY** *quickly pokes his head into the room with a lit flashlight, reacts, then exits. The* **BOYS** *giggle in the darkness.* **TED** *and* **SALLY** *appear from behind the cabins, strolling arm-in-arm down the wooded path.)*

TED. So he was just another typical big-city boy?

SALLY. Only out for himself. Rude, dishonest; great for business; not for love. Lucky for me, I got wise before it was too late.

TED. That's good. I mean, for your sake.

SALLY. And you?

TED. Well, I do this for six months out of the year; worked under Mrs. K. for a few seasons and a couple of managers before her. Odd jobs during the winter and I have plenty of time to write.

SALLY. Oooh, you still love those pulp stories; aliens and spaceships and Moon Men?

TED. Yeah, yeah, I know; kid stuff. But I actually sold a few short stories to a magazine a while back; two cents a word, but the best part was going to the newsstand and seeing my name in print.

SALLY. Yeah, I remember my first by-line. Who knew we'd both –

(at a loss for words)

#8: AND IT ALWAYS MADE YOU SMILE

TED.

WHERE DID ALL THE TIME GO?
HOW THE YEARS FLEW BY.
NEVER THOUGHT THAT I'D BE CAUGHT HERE
STILL HOME-SPUN AND SHY.

SALLY.

NEW YORK CITY'S CROWDED.
BE GLAD YOU DIDN'T LEAVE.
THE NOISE, THE STINK; IT MAKES ME THINK
HOW WE WERE SO NAÏVE.

TED.

ALL THE GUYS IN TOWN WOULD MEET
PLAYING STICK BALL IN THE STREET,
AND WHEN I WOULD HIT THAT THING A COUNTRY MILE,
FIRST I'D WATCH IT DISAPPEAR THEN TURN TO SEE YOU,
AND IT ALWAYS MADE YOU SMILE.

SALLY.

WE'D HAVE PARTIES BY THE LAKE.
ALL THE GIRLS BROUGHT TEA AND CAKE,
MAKE-BELIEVING THAT OUR DOLLS WERE DRESSED IN
   STYLE.
I PRETENDED NOT TO NOTICE WHEN YOU'D WATCH US,
AND IT ALWAYS MADE YOU SMILE.

TED.

HOLIDAYS WERE FILLED WITH LAUGHTER
AND MUSIC AND TOYS.

SALLY.

EVERYTHING FOR HAPPY YOUNG GIRLS
AND BOYS.

TED.

ALL THE BOTTOMS THAT WERE SPANKED

SALLY.

AND THE PIGTAILS THAT WERE YANKED.

BOTH.

THINGS THE ADULTS SAID WERE MEAN AND JUVENILE.

TED.

THEY WERE INNOCENT EXPRESSIONS OF AFFECTION,

SALLY.

WITHOUT A MEANINGFUL, EMOTIONAL CONNECTION,

TED.

EXCEPT ONE TIME, A KISS –

SALLY.

AND THERE WAS NO OBJECTION.

BOTH.

SO UNEXPECTED AND WORTHWHILE
AND IT ALWAYS MADE YOU SMILE.

(The music underscores as they cross to the elm tree and look at their carved initials.)

TED.

ALL THE GAMES WE PLAYED AS CHILDREN
WE SOON TIRED OF.
WAS IT BROKEN TOYS, OR BOREDOM,

SALLY.

OR LOVE?

TED.

THEN A FEW MORE YEARS WOULD PASS
AND OUR GRADUATING CLASS
FINALLY TOOK THAT LONG PROCESSION UP THE AISLE.

SALLY.

AND WE WONDERED WHO WOULD STAY AND WHO'D BE
GOING,

TED.

HOW MANY FAREWELL CELEBRATIONS WE'D BE THROWING,

BOTH.

AND WHEN WE SAID GOODBYE, WE SAID IT ALWAYS
KNOWING
AT LEAST WE HELD HANDS FOR A WHILE,
AND IT ALWAYS MADE YOU –

(As the music plays out, they look tentatively at each other, kiss, and smile.)

(After the applause, **SUSIE** *appears from under her blanket with the radio, turns it on, and we hear:)*

WOTW RADIO CUE #1. *(Announcer reports that a meteorite has crashed on a farm near Grovers Mill, New Jersey.)*
*(***IDA*** *suddenly enters and* **SUSIE** *turns the radio off.)*

IDA. *(squinting in the dark)* Is something going on in here?

GIRLS. *(quietly ad-lib)* No, Miss Rothberg –

IDA. Susie Slauson, are you playing with that radio again?

SUSIE. No, Miss Rothberg.

IDA. Go to sleep. Your parents will be here bright and early.

(returns to her room and closes the door)

(The girls ad-lib for **SUSIE** *to be quiet, but she pops her head up from under the blanket and turns the radio back on.)*

WOTW RADIO CUE #2. *(Reporter says that he and a scientist are at the farm in Grovers Mill.)*

(sound FX of random dialing)

(As **SUSIE** *turns the radio dial,* **TED** *and* **SALLY** *come up for air.)*

SALLY. That little girl's got the radio again.

TED. She loves the radio; has to fight with her brothers at home for control of the dial. Let her play. It's her last night.

(They kiss again. **SUSIE** *returns to the CBS station.*

(sound FX of random dialing)

WOTW RADIO CUE #3. *(The reporter and scientist explain that the meterorite looks like a huge metal cylinder.)*

(sound FX of random dialing)

NANCY. Susie, will you turn that thing off?

MARY. You wanna get us in trouble?

SUSIE. I lost Charlie. I can't find Charlie!

NANCY. She just doesn't get it. A ventriloquist on the radio! It's the stupidest thing I ever heard of!

SALLY. We better get inside. Someone will see.

TED. Let ME play. It's MY last night.

(The GIRLS begin to listen to the broadcast with more interest.)

(sound FX of random dialing)

WOTW RADIO CUE #4. *(The reporter explains that one end of the cylinder is unscrewing itself from the inside.)*

(sound FX of random dialing)

(IDA opens the door and turns on the lights.)

IDA. Girls!

GIRLS. Shhh!!!

SALLY. What IS she listening to in there?

(TED and SALLY move closer to the wall of the girls' cabin.)

(sound FX of random dialing)

WOTW RADIO CUE #5. *(The reporter explains that some strange creature is crawling out of the cylinder.)*

(sound FX of random dialing)

(IDA and the GIRLS squeal and ad-lib for SUSIE to stop turning the radio dial. This awakens the boys and MORTY enters the boy's cabin with his lit flashlight. TED and SALLY walk around the corner and enter the girls' cabin.)

(sound FX of random dialing)

WOTW RADIO CUE #6. *(The reporter explains how ugly and repulsive the creature is.)*

(sound FX of random dialing)

(SUSIE moves the radio closer to the end of the bed, but the cord pops out of the wall and the light and sound from the radio goes off. IDA and the GIRLS scream hysterically and all struggle to plug the cord back into the wall. MORTY and the BOYS quickly exit their cabin and look in through the window and door of the girls' cabin.

The radio goes back on and everyone sits or stands in frozen fear; sound FX of random dialing.)

WOTW RADIO CUE #7. *(Reporter hysterically explains how the creature turns a heat ray onto the innocent on-lookers, burning them and the surrounding area with sheets of fire. The reporter's transmission suddenly stops, and an announcer apologizes to the radio audience.)*

*(***TED*** switches off the radio and everyone stares silently at each other as ominous music underscores.)*

#8-A: FINALE - ACT ONE

SALLY. This can't be real.

CARL. We heard it with our own ears.

TED. I read lots of stories about Martians. I even wrote a few. But I never thought it could really happen.

NANCY. How do you know they're Martians?

TED. Well, closest planet. They're little green men of SOME kind. I don't think it matters WHERE they're from.

MORTY. They're HERE now!

NANCY. *(nudges* **SPARKY***)* Don't you have anything to say?

SPARKY. I wet my pants.

JOAN. Maybe they'll stay down by Princeton. Why would they want to invade us here?

CARL. Yeah! We haven't done anything to them!

SALLY. That's what they said in Czechoslovakia.

JOAN. Mr. Connors, what are we going to do? What about our families? What if the Martians head towards New York?

(The **KIDS** *think for a beat, then cry.* **SALLY, IDA** *and* **NANCY** *comfort them.* **TED** *herds everyone out of the girls' cabin onto the exterior path between the cabins.)*

TED. There's a telephone in Mrs. K.'s office.

SALLY. I'll call my paper. They'll know what the real scoop is on this.

IDA.

> YOU BETTER CALL WALTER WINCHELL
> YOU BETTER CALL THE F.B.I.

TEENS.

> 'CAUSE SOMETHIN' WEIRD IS UP THERE IN THE SKY.

ALL.

> OH, MY!

KIDS.

> THE BOOGEYMEN ARE GONNA GET US.
> THEY'RE GONNA SPOIL HALLOWEEN
> BY COMING DOWN HERE FROM OUTER SPACE
> IN THEIR GREAT BIG FLYING MACHINE.

> *(***MRS. K.*** enters downstage of the boys' cabin. She is wear-
> ing an improvised "Goblin" costume; green, hairy and
> scary. Her hair is tied up in a bun and she is putting on
> a hideous "Goblin" head-mask.)*

ALL.

> YOU BETTER KEEP YOUR EYES WIDE OPEN
> NO MATTER WHAT YOU DO, BEWARE!

WOMEN/GIRLS.

> THE ONE TIME WHEN YOU DON'T EXPECT IT,

MEN/BOYS.

> OOO - AH!
> YOU LOOK AWAY AND DON'T SUSPECT IT,

WOMEN / GIRLS.

> OOO - AH!

ALL.

> THE BOOGEYMAN WILL BE — RIGHT —

> *(Now in full costume, ***MRS. K.*** turns the corner and
> comes face-to-face with all the others. Screams are traded
> back and forth, then everyone scatters offstage. The
> underscoring music crashes with a very quick, loud and
> agitated playoff.)*

> *(blackout)*

End of Act One

ACT TWO

Scene One

(The Campfire; immediately following.)

#9: *LITTLE GREEN MEN*

(In the darkness after a short musical intro, we hear,)

WOTW RADIO CUE #8. *(Announcer confirms that alien creatures from the planet Mars have landed in New Jersey.)*

*(The music strikes a crashing chord and the stage lights come up. Everyone, except **MRS. K.**, screams from offstage then runs randomly in a panic throughout the campsite and the forest. When they're not scaring each other or fleeing from their own shadows, they sing to us:)*

ALL.

WE GOTTA GET AWAY BEFORE THEY COME.
NO ONE HAS ANY IDEA WHAT WE'RE RUNNING FROM.
BUT WE ARE SAFE IN ASSUMIN' THEY'RE NOT EVEN HUMAN,
THOSE LITTLE GREEN MEN FROM MARS.

WHAT ARE THEY LANDING IN NEW JERSEY FOR?
IT SEEMS LIKE A STUPID PLACE TO TRY AND START A WAR
AND CAUSE THE ANNIHILATION OF CIVILIZATION
BY THOSE LITTLE GREEN MEN FROM MARS.

    WHAT DO THEY WANT? WHAT DO THEY WANT?
    WHAT DO THEY WANT
    FROM OUR PLEASANT PEACEFUL PLANET?
    ALL THAT WE KNOW, ALL THAT WE KNOW
    IT WASN'T US WHO BEGAN IT.

THEY COME FROM SEV'RAL MILLION MILES AWAY,
BUT THEY ARE NOT ON VACATION, THEY ARE HERE TO STAY.

THIS SUDDEN SURPRISE ARRIVAL COULD END OUR
   SURVIVAL
THANKS TO LITTLE GREEN MEN –
LITTLE GREEN MEN FROM MARS.

(As the panic continues, **MRS. K.***, still dressed as the
"Goblin," steps out from the bushes. Every time she tries
to scare someone, they are already running from a previ-
ous scare elsewhere and pass by her without looking. She
takes off her mask and looks back and forth, scratching
her head, puzzled as to why everyone is ignoring her. She
puts the mask back on and disappears into the forest, as
smaller groups move downstage and sing.)*

ALL.

WHERE DO WE GO? WHERE DO WE HIDE?
HOW DO WE SAVE OURSELVES?
DO WE GIVE IN OR GIVE THEM A FIGHT?

*(As the screaming and running continues onstage and
off,* **TED**, **SALLY** *and* **IDA** *meet center stage, as the music
underscores.)*

TED. Did you see any of them?

IDA. The Martians?

TED. The kids! We've got to get everyone under control. If
any of them get hurt out here, their parents will sue
the pants off us!

IDA. *(hysterical)* Does that really matter considering it's the
END OF THE WORLD??

TED. Ida, get a hold of yourself.

(slaps her forcefully)

We have to be the mature adults. We have to set a calm
and rational example for those poor frightened children.

*(***MORTY** *runs across the stage, screaming.)*

SALLY. *(also hysterical)* And we can't find Mrs. Kolotsky!!

*(***TED** *motions to slap her, but she defends herself with a
raised fist and a defiant glare.)*

IDA. Didja look UNDER the desk in her office?

SALLY. She's not there. And we can't call out on the telephone. All we get are busy signals.

TED. Round everybody up and let's meet in the dining hall. I'll get the radio. We've still got power. Maybe they're still broadcasting.

*(**MORTY** runs across again with a squirrel on the back of his neck. **IDA** chases after him as **TED** and **SALLY** run off in the opposite direction.)*

*(Smaller groups of **TEENS**, **KIDS** and **ADULTS** continue to run back and forth through the campsite as they sing.)*

ALL.

SUPPOSE THEY KNOW HOW TO CONTROL OUR BRAINS,
THEN LIKE A VAMPIRE SUCK THE BLOOD OUT FROM OUR
    VEINS.
AND WE WOULD BE NONE THE WISER; A QUICK APPETIZER,
FOR THOSE LITTLE GREEN MEN FROM MARS.

SUPPOSE THEY HAVE A TASTE FOR LIVING FLESH
AND THEY KNOW HOW TO FLAMBEE US OR FILLET US
    FRESH,
OR MAYBE THEY'LL FRICASSEE US THE MINUTE THEY SEE
    US,
THOSE LITTLE GREEN MEN FROM MARS.

WHY DO THEY WANT, WHY DO THEY WANT,
WHY DO THEY WANT
TO ATTACK AND SMASH OUR HEAD IN?
IS IT THE TIME, IS IT THE TIME,
IS IT TIME FOR ARMAGEDDON?

OUR MILITARY DOESN'T HAVE A CHANCE
AGAINST THOSE INVADERS CRUSHING US LIKE TINY ANTS.
WE'RE GETTING BATTERED AND BEATEN AND WORST OF
    ALL, EATEN
BY THOSE LITTLE GREEN MEN –
LITTLE GREEN MEN –
LITTLE GREEN MEN – FROM MARS!

*(As the groups disperse, **MRS. K.** enters from the bushes
and tries once again to scare somebody, but they all run
right past her. She removes her mask, shrugs in resigna-
tion, and walks offstage.)*

(blackout)

#9-A: SCENE CHANGE

Scene Two

(The Dining Hall; immediately following; lit only by the moonlight through the windows, the main door and the kitchen door open slowly at the same time. **MORTY** *and* **IDA** *with their lit flashlights cautiously back in from each door, then bump back-to-back at center. They scream and run to the light switches by both doors, alternately turning them on-and-off quickly. Finally when they recognize each other, they run and embrace at center stage.)*

IDA. Jeez, I thought you were the Martian!

MORTY. Me, too! The shadows were so spooky. All I could see was this squat, hideous thing with ears out to here and a nose out to –

IDA. Alright, alright! There weren't *that* many shadows!

MORTY. Honest, baby, I didn't know it was you. Now that thing we saw out by the cabins, *that* was a Martian!

IDA. Everybody started screaming. I didn't know what it was!

MORTY. It was big and ugly; could've been a bear or a moose –

IDA. Or the Goblin!

MORTY. The Goblin is a moose??

IDA. Or the Martian is the Goblin! Oh, Morty, I am so scared! I want to get out of here tonight!

MORTY. Don't worry, baby. I won't let anything happen to you.

*(**MORTY** crosses to her, trips, and she catches him.)*

IDA. *(sarcastically)* I feel so safe.

MORTY. You should! On the outside, I might look like a bumbling sidekick. But inside –

(strikes a heroic pose)

#10: I WILL BE YOUR HERO

MORTY. *(cont.)*
ROBIN HOOD!

IDA. Knock on wood.

MORTY.
IVANHOE!

IDA. I don't know.

MORTY.
CHARLES DARNAY!

IDA. Not today.

MORTY.
SIR LANCELOT!

IDA. No, thanks a lot.

MORTY.
DANIEL BOONE!

IDA. No time soon.

MORTY.
ULYSSES GRANT.

IDA. No, I can't!

MORTY.
WHAT DO THESE GREAT MEN GOT
THAT MORTY KLEIN'S NOT – GOT?

IDA. Well, if I have to spell it out for ya –
IF THE MARTIANS COME TO GET ME,
DO I NEED TO FEAR?

MORTY.
OHHH, MEN FROM MARS WON'T BOTHER US
'CAUSE I WILL BE YOUR HERO.

IDA.
IF THEY ZAP ME WITH THEIR RAY GUNS,
AND I DISAPPEAR,

MORTY.
OHHH, THEY AIN'T ZAPPIN' ANYONE
'CAUSE I WILL BE YOUR HERO.

IDA.

> WILL THEY DESTROY OUR NATION
> LIKE SOME SABOTAGERS COULD?

MORTY.

> I'LL FIGHT OFF THEIR INVASION
> JUST THE WAY BUCK ROGERS WOULD.

IDA.

> AREN'T THEY SLIMY, GOOEY CREATURES,
> ALL DEFORMED AND QUEER?

MORTY.

> OHHH, YOU WON'T EVER HAVE TO SEE A
> THING WITH SOME DEFORMITY
> UNLESS YOU'RE LOOKIN' STRAIGHT AT ME
> 'CAUSE I WILL BE YOUR HERO.

> *(dance sequence, then:)*

IDA.

> SUPPOSE OUR GUNS ARE TOYS
> AGAINST THEIR MARTIAN ARSENALS?

MORTY.

> THEN I WILL MAKE SOME NOISE
> BY "YULLING" JUST LIKE TARZAN "YULLS."

> *(He beats his chest and yells meekly, and they finish their dance; then:)*

IDA.

> EVERY DAMSEL IN DISTRESS
> NEEDS SOME PATHETIC PUTZ
> TO RESCUE HER WHEN SHE GETS IN A JAM.

MORTY.

> DESPITE THE DANGER, NONETHELESS,
> HE GOES COMPLETELY NUTS
> JUST TO GET THAT GRATEFUL KISS, AND HERE I AM.

IDA.

> CAN'T THEY JUST OBSERVE US
> FROM THE UPPER ATMOSPHERE?

MORTY.

> OHHH, MARTIANS WANT A REAL GOOD LOOK,
> BUT I WILL BE YOUR HERO.

IDA.

> CAN'T WE HIDE UNTIL THE ARMY
> SAYS THE COAST IS CLEAR?

MORTY.

> OHHH, YOU DON'T NEED AN ARMY, HONEY.
> I WILL BE YOUR HERO.

IDA.

> SUPPOSE THEY TRY TO COOK US
> LIKE A CHICKEN CORDON BLEU?

MORTY.

> THEN I WILL KICK THEM IN THE TUCHAS
> LIKE FLASH GORDON DO.

IDA.

> WHY DON'T THEY GO BACK TO MARS
> AND STAY AWAY FROM HERE?

MORTY.

> OHHH, MAYBE THEY ARE JUST LIKE ME
> AND WANT TO BE CLOSE AS CAN BE
> TO THE SWEETEST GAL IN ALL NEW JERSEY.

IDA. Aww, Morty!

MORTY.	**IDA.**
I WILL BE	
YOUR HERO –	MY HERO –

(pose, embrace, kiss)

#10-A: *I WILL BE YOUR HERO; encore*

IDA.

> LADIES NEVER LIKE IT IF
> THEY'RE LAYING ON THEIR BACKS
> AND MOVING TOWARDS A BUZZ SAW AS IT SPINS.

MORTY.

> BUT CLINGING TO A ROCKY CLIFF
> OR TIED TO RAILROAD TRACKS,
> THEY KNOW, IN THE END, THE HERO ALWAYS WINS.

IDA.

> IF WE NEED SOME VIGILANTES,
> WILL YOU VOLUNTEER?

MORTY.

> OH, I'LL BE THERE WITH GUNS A-BLAZIN'.
> I WILL BE YOUR HERO.

IDA.

> CAN'T THEY JUST DRIVE BY AND WAVE
> AND TAKE A SOUVENIR?

MORTY.

> OH, MEN FROM MARS AIN'T HERE FOR TCHOTCHKIES.
> I WILL BE YOUR HERO.

IDA.

> YOU SAY THE WAR THEY'RE BRINGING
> SHOULD NOT WORRY ME BECAUSE?

MORTY.

> I'LL SEND 'EM ALL TO SING SING
> JUST THE WAY DICK TRACY DOES.

IDA.

> WHY DON'T THEY GO BACK TO MARS
> AND STAY AWAY FROM HERE?

MORTY.

> OH, MAYBE THEY ARE JUST LIKE ME
> AND WANT TO BE CLOSE AS CAN BE
> TO THE SWEETEST GAL IN ALL NEW JERSEY.

IDA. Aww, you said it again!

MORTY.	**IDA.**
I WILL BE –	
YOUR HERO!	MY HERO!

*(After the applause, **MRS. K.**, still wearing her "Goblin" costume and carrying the head in one hand, stumbles in backwards through the main door. **MORTY** and **IDA** scream and run out through the kitchen door. **MRS. K.** turns, struggling to reach the upper back of her costume with her other hand.)*

MRS. K. Ohh, why me! Why now! Darn zipper is stuck. Won't budge – awww –

*(**MRS. K.** stumbles into the picnic table and howls in pain just as **CARL**, **JOAN** and the **KIDS** open the main door. They see "The Martian" wailing, scream and run back outside through the main door.)*

I can't have anyone see me like THIS!

*(**MRS. K.** staggers out through the kitchen door, still awkwardly struggling with the zipper. **CARL** bursts through the main door, yelling and waving a baseball bat. **JOAN** and the **KIDS** poke their heads in at the door.)*

MARY. Where is it?

GEORGIE. We saw it. Right there!

SUSIE. Where did it go?

JOEY. Back to Mars, I hope.

JOAN. Well, it's gone for now. Everyone get inside.

*(The **KIDS** follow **JOAN** inside.)*

CARL. The adults must be looking for us. We'll keep the lights on so they'll know we're here.

MARY. I'm cold.

GEORGIE. I'm hungry.

JOEY. I'm scared.

SUSIE. I'm short.

*(The **KIDS** sit at the table.)*

CARL. Try to stay calm, kids. Ted and Ida and Morty and Sally are our friends. They wouldn't leave us here alone.

*(The **KIDS** cry and wail.)*

Look, this doesn't make any sense. That thing we saw, it couldn't have been a Martian! The radio said the spaceship landed way south of here. How could it get here that fast?

JOAN. Well, it got here fast enough from Mars! What's a little hop and a skip from Grovers Mill? Boing! Boing! Arrggg!!

(The **KIDS** *cry some more.)*

CARL. No, think about it. One single Martian wandering around on his own up here in the woods? What kind of invasion is that? I don't think it was a Martian at all.

JOAN. Then it must have been the Goblin!

(The **KIDS** *cry even louder.)*

CARL. *(aside to* **JOAN***)* Will you stop HELPING me? I'm trying to keep them quiet.

JOAN. Oh, right. Gee, Carl, you're so smart.

*(***CARL** *and* **JOAN** *sit with the* **KIDS** *at the table, comforting them.)*

CARL. It's OK, Mary. You'll see. We'll all be back home in the morning just like Mrs. K. promised.

MARY. Where *is* Mrs. K.? Did she leave us alone, too?

CARL. No, no. I'm sure she's out there like everyone else, looking for us.

JOAN. See? Look how good you are with kids. You'd make a terrific father.

(Caught in a moment of weakness, **CARL** *gives* **JOAN** *a perturbed look and stands. There's a crashing sound from inside the kitchen and* **CARL** *grabs the baseball bat.)*

CARL. That does it! Martian or Goblin or whatever the heck you are, prepare to meet the revenge of Carl Leslie Bennett, the Third!

JOAN & KIDS. "Leslie??!"

CARL. No time for that now. This is man's work!

*(***CARL** *storms off into the kitchen waving the baseball bat.* **JOEY** *and* **GEORGIE** *run up to the kitchen door, imitating* **CARL***.)*

JOEY & GEORGIE. This is man's work!

(They storm off into the kitchen. There's more loud crashing, then the two **BOYS** *quickly return, breathing hard, scared to death. They look at the girls, take a deep breath, a manly stance, then run back into the kitchen.)*

MARY. Aren't they wonderful?

SUSIE. Laughing in the face of danger, just like Errol Flynn.

JOAN. *(touched by* **CARL***'s bravery)* Braving the unknown to save us poor girls from certain death.

SUSIE. Really? CERTAIN death?

SUSIE & MARY. Wow!

JOAN. Well, certain or not, it's the thought that counts. They just automatically wanted to help us.

MARY. Hey, Joanie, maybe boys aren't so bad after all.

*(**SUSIE** looks at **MARY**, her jaw dropping, shocked that Mary would admit such a thing.)*

#11: FOR EVERY GIRL, THERE'S ONE GUY

JOAN.

EVERY GIRL DREAMS OF SOME GUY COMPLETING HER PLAN,
AND FOR EVERY GIRL THERE'S ONE GUY WHO CAN.
EVERY GIRL WANTS HER CASTLE BUILT HIGH ON A HILL,
AND FOR EVERY GIRL THERE'S ONE GUY WHO WILL.

SOME WILL ADORE YOU, SOME WILL DECEIVE.
SOME WILL BE TOO POLITE.
OTHERS WILL BORE YOU, OTHERS WILL LEAVE,
'TIL ONE DAY THERE'S ONE WHO'S RIGHT.

EVERY GIRL WANTS PRINCE CHARMING TO CLAIM HER AS HIS,
AND FOR EVERY GIRL THERE'S ONE GUY,
EVENTUALLY SHE FINDS THAT ONE GUY,
AND FOR EVERY GIRL THERE'S ONE GUY WHO IS.

SUSIE. Is this one of those things we should remember when we grow up?

JOAN. It couldn't hurt.

MARY & SUSIE. O.K.

ALL.

EVERY GIRL DREAMS OF SOME GUY COMPLETING HER PLAN,
AND FOR EVERY GIRL THERE'S ONE GUY WHO CAN.

MARY & SUSIE.

AHHH.

ALL.

> EVERY GIRL WANTS HER CASTLE BUILT HIGH ON A HILL,
> AND FOR EVERY GIRL THERE'S ONE GUY WHO WILL.

MARY & SUSIE.

> AHHH.

JOAN.

> SOME WILL ADORE YOU,

MARY. Jimmy Franconi; sits behind me at school; can't take his eyes off me.

JOAN.

> SOME WILL DECEIVE.

SUSIE. Gary Stiglitz; gives me an unwrapped box of Cracker Jack with the prize missing; not a chance!

JOAN.

> SOME WILL BE TOO POLITE.

MARY & SUSIE. Joey DeLuca!

JOAN.

> OTHERS WILL BORE YOU,

MARY & SUSIE. Joey DeLuca!

JOAN.

> OTHERS WILL LEAVE,

MARY. Marty Pudzer; he leaves the classroom every hour to go tinkle. His thingy must be broken.

JOAN.

> 'TIL ONE DAY THERE'S ONE WHO'S RIGHT.

(A pair of snuggling squirrels and raccoons appear in the windows.)

ALL.

> EVERY GIRL WANTS PRINCE CHARMING TO CLAIM HER AS HIS,
> AND FOR EVERY GIRL THERE'S ONE GUY,

JOAN.

> EVENTUALLY SHE FINDS THAT ONE GUY,

ALL.

> AND FOR EVERY GIRL THERE'S ONE GUY WHO IS.

(After the applause, **TED, SALLY, SPARKY** *and* **NANCY** *enter through the main door, which frightens away the squirrels and raccoons.* **TED** *carries the radio and everybody comforts each other ad-lib.)*

TED. Alright, where are the boys?

MARY. Out back, laughing in the face of danger.

SUSIE. And saving us from certain death.

(takes radio from **TED** *and plugs it into the wall by the table)*

JOAN. They're chasing something they heard rattling through the kitchen.

*(***TED** *exits quickly into the kitchen.)*

NANCY. Oh, honey, did that nasty Martian take a bite out of you?

JOAN. We're fine, really. But Carl says it's not a Martian at all.

SPARKY. What I saw was big and green and ugly! That's good enough for me.

*(***MORTY** *and* **IDA** *enter through the main door.)*

IDA. We saw it, too!

MORTY. It was right here in this room, not ten minutes ago!

MARY. Did you see it, really? Close up?

MORTY. You remember Miss Rothberg first thing in the morning at reveille?

MARY. Scarier that THAT?

IDA. Hey!

*(***TED** *returns from the kitchen as* **SUSIE** *starts dialing on the radio)*

SALLY. Listen!

NANCY. That's not the right station.

JOAN. Yeah, put on the program we heard before.

SALLY. That's my point. It was only a program. Why would all these other stations still be broadcasting if the country was under attack?

TED. She's right.

SPARKY. You mean it was a fake broadcast?

SALLY. It has to be! That voice! I knew I recognized it from somewhere! It's that darn Orson Welles and his radio show!

NANCY. A radio show?

SALLY. Mercury Theatre something. Every Sunday night at 8:00. Columbia Broadcasting out of New York. Here, Susie, let me.

(*sound FX of random dialing*)

(**SALLY** *turns the radio dial until we hear,*)

WOTW RADIO CUE #9. (*Announcer makes a formal disclaimer that the program is a fictional dramatic presentation and not an actual invasion.*)

(**SALLY** *turns off the radio.*)

SUSIE. I toldja we shoulda listened to Charlie.

TED. A bunch of radio actors doing a play. And we fell for it.

SPARKY. How do you like that!

SALLY. Thousands of people around the country are listening to this show and if they didn't hear the introduction, same as us, THEY ain't gonna like it either. Wow, what a story!

JOAN. Then the world ISN'T coming to an end. Everything's going to be O.K.

(*Ad-lib cheering from everyone.* **CARL** *enters through the kitchen door holding the "Goblin" mask at arm's length in front of him.* **JOEY** *and* **GEORGIE** *follow.* **IDA** *screams at the mask.*)

CARL. Look what I found out by the office.

JOAN. Carl! You killed the Martian! Oh, you're wonderful.

CARL. It's a mask, Joanie! A Halloween mask, and a real cheap one, at that!

TED. Where did you find it?

JOEY. In the trash can by Mrs. K.'s office.

GEORGIE. We chased a big ol' raccoon out of the kitchen and it knocked the can over and we found this on the inside.

SUSIE. A real raccoon??

*(**TED** moves **SUSIE** and **GEORGIE** out of the way towards the window.)*

NANCY. But that's the Martian. Why would a Martian be wearing a mask?

SALLY. There isn't any Martian!

MARY. Then it was the Goblin wearing a Martian mask!

MORTY. *(to **IDA**)* Don't forget about the moose!

CARL. There isn't any Martian and there isn't any Goblin! It's Mrs. Kolotsky!

ALL. *(ad-lib, great confusion)* Mrs. Kolotsky is a Martian?? — A Goblin?? – A monster??

MORTY. Kolotsky's a moose??

*(**SUSIE** and **GEORGIE** cross down, pulling on **TED**'s sleeve.)*

SUSIE. Can we catch the raccoon and keep it?

*(**TED** pushes them towards the window again.)*

SPARKY. Carl, how do you know it was Mrs. K.?

CARL. Is there anyone else up here besides us?

(holds up mask)

SPARKY. *(sniffs mask)* Wooo. That's Mrs. Kolotsky's perfume, all right.

SALLY. My hunch was right. Mrs. K. wants this property for herself and *she* started those Gitchiegoomie Goblin rumors so parents would stop sending their kids here for camp and push the property value into a nose dive.

IDA. Oh! That's terrible!

TED. Now, wait. Mrs. K. *is* a bit eccentric, but I've worked with her for years. Maybe she was just dressing up to get into the Halloween spirit.

CARL. I also found *these* in the trash can.

(shows objects in hand)

SPARKY. Spark plugs! These are the spark plugs for the bus!

IDA. *(to MORTY)* You didn't check the spark plugs??

(punches his arm)

JOAN. What does that mean, Carl?

TED. Mrs. Kolotsky purposely disabled the bus so we'd be stuck here tonight and she could give us a good scare –

SALLY. – and you'd all go home tomorrow and tell your parents and friends to never come here again! Then she gets the Board to sell her this land for next to nothing! What a scandal! This'll be front page headlines. If only I could get through on that telephone!

TED. Sally, we can't prove anything. A Halloween mask and some spark plugs aren't enough to connect Mrs. K. to anything dishonest.

MORTY. We need some hard evidence against the old bat.

IDA. Something we can testify with in court.

(SUSIE and GEORGIE cross away excitedly from the window.)

GEORGIE. She's coming! She's coming down the path from the office.

TED. Alright, campers. How'd you like to play one last game?

(TEENS & KIDS ad-lib excitedly.)

Mrs. K. likes to scare little kids on Halloween. How about we give her a taste of her own medicine?

TEENS & KIDS. Hooray!!!

TED. Shhh!

TEENS & KIDS. *(very softly)* Hooray –

(Everyone exits quickly through the main door. **MRS. K.** *pokes her head in through the kitchen door. She is wearing her regular clothes.)*

MRS. K. Hello? Hello, anybody here?

(searches about the room)

Are you hiding from me? Is somebody going to jump out at me and say "Boo?"

(claps her hands, satisfied that she is alone)

Aha! I did it! They're gone. Not a scream to be heard for miles. Right now they're tumbling down that road in the dark! Ha-ha-ha –

(turns on the radio and does a little victory dance step to the music that plays softly, then exits into the kitchen.)

#12: NO MORE

(The **ADULTS, TEENS & KIDS** *poke their heads in through the main door and the windows as the music underscores quietly.)*

TED. Everybody hear that?

(Others agree ad-lib.)

SALLY. Ted, what are you planning to do?

TED. How about we do to her what Orson Welles did to us?

SALLY. But it's after nine o'clock. His broadcast is over.

TED. We're a couple of writers; GOOD writers. We'll make it up as we go!

(to the others)

OK. Meet us up by the cabins. And be quiet. Don't let her see you. And Susie – you're in charge of the radio.

SUSIE. Yes, sir, Mr. Connors!

*(***SUSIE*** hides behind some boxes in the corner within arm's reach of the radio on the table. The* **ADULTS, TEENS & KIDS** *disappear as* **MRS. K.** *enters from the kitchen with a tray of sandwiches, cheese and a bottle*

of wine. She puts the tray on the picnic table and starts nibbling and sipping as she moves to the Latin samba music coming from the radio.)

MRS. K.

ALL OF THE THINGS I WANTED WILL START TO HAPPEN.
I'LL BE IN CHARGE THE WAY THAT IT OUGHT TO BE.
I RAN THIS SUMMER CAMP INTO THE SKIDS.
I'LL BUY IT BACK BEFORE SOMEBODY BIDS.
AND THERE'LL BE NO MORE NASTY LITTLE KIDS FOR ME.

SOON I CAN BUILD MY PRIVATE ADULT OASIS
ONLY FOR MEMBERS WHO CAN AFFORD THE FEE.
THOSE BIG REPUBLICANS AND DEMOCRATS
WILL COME TO SHED THEIR CALORIES AND FATS
AND THERE'LL BE NO MORE NOISY LITTLE BRATS FOR ME.

ROOSEVELTS WILL PLAY WITH THE MORGANS,
WAVING TO POSSUMS AND SQUIRRELS
WHILE I'M GETTING RICH MASSAGING THEIR FLABBY
    ORGANS.
SO NO MORE NAUGHTY BOYS AND GIRLS FOR ME.

(Music plays as she drinks from the wine bottle.)

I'll burn all these log cabins right to the ground.

(Music plays as she rips a few drawings and decorations from the wall.)

Arts and crafts – garbage!

(Music plays as she dances and destroys a few more items that the campers created.)

SNOBS FROM NEW YORK'S UPPER CLASSES,
BORED WITH THEIR AIRPLANES AND YACHTS,
WILL PAY ME TO SHRINK THEIR OVER-INFLATED ASSES.
SO NO MORE NEEDY LITTLE TOTS FOR ME.

(As **MRS. K.** *sips more wine, the music vamps.* **TED** *peeks in from one of the windows and signals* **SUSIE** *to turn off the volume on the radio. She does, and* **TED** *speaks like a radio announcer, cupping his hand to his ear.)*

TED. We interrupt this program for an emergency news announcement. Scientists at Princeton University in Princeton have just reported a huge fireball from outer space has crashed in the area of northwestern New Jersey.

*(***MRS. K.*** *does a huge spit-take.)*

Please keep listening to this station for further developments.

*(On ***TED****'s signal, ***SUSIE*** turns up the volume on the radio, turns the dial and we hear the opening chords of Grieg's Piano Concerto. Lit candelabras appear in the windows. ***MRS. K.*** reacts to the new music coming from the radio, then continues singing.)*

MRS. K.

CAMP GITCHIEGOOMIE, PLAYGROUND FOR THE POOR,
MEANS NOTHING TO ME; I CLOSE THE IRON DOOR.
EVERY YEAR, I'M STUCK HERE,
SUPERVISING A COUPLE OF HUNDRED CHILDREN.

*(The candelabras disappear as ***SUSIE*** turns the radio dial again and we hear a big band playing something that sounds like "Sing, Sing, Sing.")*

EAT, EAT, EAT, EAT.
ALL THEY WANT TO DO IS EAT.
THEY GO FOR SECONDS AND FOR THIRDS,
THEN TRY TO SNEAK A SNACK IN AFTERWARDS.

*(Music continues as ***TED****,* ***SALLY****,* ***MORTY*** *and* ***IDA*** *enter through the doors dressed as zoot suited jitterbugging dancers. ***MRS. K.****, drunk from the wine, isn't sure if they are real or hallucinations.)*

EAT, EAT, EAT, EAT.
I CAN BARELY MAKE ENDS MEET.
WITH WHAT IT COSTS TO FEED 'EM ALL,
I COULD LIVE INSIDE THE TAJ MAHAL.

*(***TED****,* ***SALLY****,* ***MORTY*** *and* ***IDA*** *exit.)*

But thanks to me and the ol' Goblin, this place is worthless!

(SUSIE turns the radio dial again and we hear a polka band.)

MRS. K. *(cont.)*

    IF THEY DON'T WANT IT, I WILL TAKE IT.

    IT'S O.K. FOR ME.

    YAH, IT'S O.K. FOR ME, YAH, IT'S O.K. FOR ME.

    IF THEY WILL SELL IT, I WILL BUY IT.

    IT'S O.K. FOR ME.

    YAH, IT'S O.K., IT'S O.K., IT'S O.K. FOR ME.

(TED and SALLY enter as a happy Tyrolian couple and polka around the room as MORTY enters playing a small accordion and IDA enters as a German barmaid with blonde braided hair, waving a beer stein. They exit.)

Oh, I'll have swimming pools – a tennis court –

(suggestively)

– a tennis instructor!

(SUSIE turns radio dial again and we hear the Latin samba music. TED, SALLY, MORTY and IDA enter as Spanish dancers behind MRS. K.)

MRS. K.	**TED, SALLY, MORTY, IDA.**
CHILDREN ARE FUN IN	
SMALL DOSES.	
IT'S DAY AFTER DAY THAT	
ANNOYS.	HASTA LA VISTA.
I'VE SAID MY "GOODBYES,"	GOODBYES,
"ADIOS" AND "ADIOSES."	ADIOSES –.
CAMP GITCHIEGOOMIE	
SOON WILL BE	
BIG ROTTING PILES OF	
DEBRIS.	
NO MORE LITTLE GIRLS	NO MORE GIRLS AND BOYS
AND BOYS – FOR – ME –.	– FOR – ME –.

MRS. K. *(like Señor Wences)* 'salright?

TED, SALLY, MORTY, IDA. 'salright!

    (exit)

*(After the applause, **TED** appears at one of the windows, signals **SUSIE** to turn off the radio and speaks again like an announcer.)*

TED. We interrupt our program once again for this emergency announcement. It's been confirmed that the giant fireball from outer space has landed in the woods near Camp Gitchiegoomie –

*(**MRS. K.** gasps and clutches her chest.)*

– a privately-funded wilderness retreat for inner city boys and girls.

MRS. K. Not for long!

(looks out the main door)

TED. We now have a report from our field correspondent, Lucille Hassenfeffer, who is in the field at the crash sight with an eyewitness account of the crash. Take it away, Lucille.

*(**SALLY**'s head appears in the window next to **TED**.)*

SALLY. *(to **TED**, annoyed)* "Lucille??"

*(**TED** prompts her to continue.)*

Thank you – Sheldon! Yes, I'm here on the south ridge near Camp Gitchiegoomie. The object is glowing a bright red and orange. It's lighting up the entire night sky.

*(**MRS. K.** takes a pair of Army binoculars off the shelf and looks outside the main door.)*

The strangest thing is, it doesn't look like a meteor at all — at least not like any other meteor I've seen. It's shiny and smooth and looks more like a – like a big swollen jelly bean stuck in the mud.

TED. It looks like a what?

SALLY. Never mind, Sheldon! Something's happening. Can you hear that? Some kind of strange sound is coming from the object!

*(**MORTY** pokes his head up in the other window.)*

TED. You mean the big jelly bean?

SALLY. I said, a strange sound is coming from the object.

MORTY. *(like a cow)* Moo!

SALLY. No, I think it's more of a mechanical sound.

> **(IDA** *pokes her head up next to* **MORTY,** *punches his arm and together they make more mechanical-like sounds. They duck out of sight as* **MRS. K.** *looks out the window, then reappear as she moves to the other window.* **TED** *and* **SALLY** *duck out of sight, then* **MRS. K.** *moves away from that window and they reappear.)*

TED. Ah, yes! I hear it now. Sounds like Dr. Frankenstein's laboratory.

> **(MORTY** *gets carried away with the sound effects.)*

SALLY. OK, I think it's stopped now.

MORTY. *(in a Colin Clive voice)* It's alive! It's alive!! It's alive –

> *(cackles like Igor and grunts like the Monster)*

SALLY. Yes, the sounds have stopped now!

> **(IDA** *pulls* **MORTY** *below the window and he smacks his chin on the sill as he disappears.)*

Oh! This is incredible. The top of the object is unscrewing itself – from the inside.

> **(MRS. K.** *sits on a crate next to the radio, listening intently.)*

There's something INSIDE that object trying to get out! A hideous living creature, obviously not of this earth, is starting to climb towards us.

TED. Lucille, that sounds absolutely amazing.

SALLY. Well, Sheldon, it is. Oh! I can't look!

TED. But you must look, Lucille. You must. Tell the people of America what is happening there in the wilds of New Jersey.

MRS. K. *(to the radio)* Yes, tell us! I can't see a thing!!

SALLY. Wait! Here's someone! Maybe he saw the fireball come down. He appears to be a local farmer; old man, toothless, smells of freshly mown hay. Says his name is Hootchins.

MRS. K. *(to the radio)* Hootkins!!

SALLY. Hootkins! Mr. Hootkins, what can you tell us about this catastrophe?

(**MORTY** *and* **IDA** *reappear in their window and she nudges him.*)

MORTY. *(in a Percy Kilbride voice)* Me and the missus was a-sittin' down to supper when –

TED. Can you get to the point, Mr. Hootkins? This could be the end of the world here!

MORTY. Alright, sonny, don't rush me. I'm an old man, you know. And toothless.

SALLY. What can you tell us about this Camp Gitchiegoomie?

MORTY. I hear tell they have a wonderful staff of workers there.

MRS. K. Ha!

IDA. Eeee-yup.

SALLY. And who's that, Mr. Hootkins?

MORTY. Sadie.

SALLY. Sadie?

MORTY. Ma mule.

(**IDA** *punches* **MORTY**'*s arm.*)

Ma wife. That's the missus. Sadie Hootkins.

IDA. *(in a Marjorie Main voice)* Eee-yup. But that old battle axe who runs the place – she's a terror.

(**MRS. K.** *is shocked.*)

MORTY. Waters down the soup, hates children and goes through their pockets at night for loose change.

MRS. K. *(to the radio)* Hootkins! You liar!!

TED. Lucille, we just got a report from the scientists at Princeton. The big jelly beans are falling all over the country and it appears to be a full-scale invasion from the planet Mars.

SALLY. You mean little green men?

TED. And you know what they say about little green men!

MRS. K. *(to the radio)* What?? What do they say??

MORTY. *(sings)* "They come from several million miles away –"

(IDA pulls MORTY out of sight banging his chin again.)

SALLY. More of these hideous Martians are surrounding a large building in the middle of Camp Gitchiegoomie. Could anyone still be in there? They're right behind me! Ahhhhhh!!

(TED and SALLY disappear below the windowsill.)

MRS. K. *(leaps away from the radio)* Ahhhhhh!!

(CARL and SPARKY enter from the kitchen as JOAN and NANCY enter through the main door. They are disguised as two-headed Martians, each couple wearing green bed sheets and blankets from the cabins like big tunics with strips of the cabin curtains tied around their waists as belts. They also wear some of Ida's hair curlers, cold cream and sleeping masks, and hold metal kitchen utensils as "hands." They flicker the room lights a few times, then surround MRS. K. at center. TED, SALLY, MORTY and IDA make weird outer space noises from offstage.)

TEENS. *(in nasal alien-like voices)* Ko-lot-sky. Ko-lot-sky. Ko-lot-sky –

MRS. K. Stay away from me!! Don't you touch me!!

SPARKY. You are the human called Kolotsky?

CARL, JOAN & NANCY. Ko-lot-sky.

MRS. K. What??

JOAN. Your reputation has spread throughout the galaxy.

NANCY. You are bad to Earth children. You take the money from their sponsors and spend it on yourself.

MRS. K. What??

NANCY. We know all and see all.

MRS. K. How dare you accuse me!

SPARKY. You never buy new sports equipment or finger paints or fresh blankets for the Earth children in your care.

MRS. K. There's nothing wrong with those blankets. We've used them for years.

JOAN. So you confess?

MRS. K. I confess nothing, not to a bunch of stinking creatures from Mars.

SPARKY. We do not stink, Kolotsky. It is you who stink.

CARL. And the blankets!

NANCY. Who told you we are from Mars?

MRS. K. The radio!

SPARKY. Uh-oh! They are on to us!

NANCY. We must hurry and complete our mission.

MRS. K. Help! Get me out of here!!

TEENS. Confess – confess – confess –

> *(As the* **TEENS** *circle* **MRS. K.,** *she crouches on top of the picnic table.* **JOEY, GEORGIE** *and* **MARY** *enter through both doors, also disguised as Martians and walking on their knees.)*

TEENS & KIDS. Confess – confess – confess –

#12-A: CONFESSION

MRS. K. Alright! I confess! I confess everything! I was the Gitchiegoomie Goblin!

> *(music sting)*

I scared everyone away so the Board of Directors would sell me this land.

> *(music sting)*

I've been embezzling from the accounts for years!

> *(music sting)*

MRS. K. *(cont.)* And, yes, – I hate children!!

(Music sting and the **KIDS** *faint on the floor.)*

I've always hated children!! Every last one of them! But you little green men will never take me alive! Ha-ha-ha!

*(***MRS. K.*** *forces her way to the main door as* **TED**, **MORTY** *and* **IDA** *enter from the kitchen, laughing. The* **TEENS & KIDS** *laugh with them as they remove their disguises and* **SUSIE** *crosses next to the group.* **MRS. K.** *turns in the doorway, realizes the truth, and tries to play along.)*

Oh! How could you! Mr. Connors! Mr. Klein! That's quite a Halloween prank to pull on an old lady with a weak heart. For a minute there I actually believed –

MORTY. *(in an Oliver Hardy voice)* You certainly did!

MRS. K. Well, we've all had our fun –

TED. No more fun, Mrs. K. and no more lies. We all heard your confession and I'll bring every one of these kids into court to testify if I have to.

MRS. K. You think I was serious? I was just playing along. Why, I would –

IDA. You can't get out of this one, Kolotsky.

MORTY. We've got you dead to rights.

(shows her the spark plugs)

You're outta here on the six A.M. bus straight to Palookaville!

MRS. K. This is ridiculous; a bunch of menials and layabouts and useless children. You can't pin anything on ME. I'll deny everything.

*(***SALLY*** *enters from the kitchen carrying two account books.)*

SALLY. Deny *this*, Kolotsky.

MRS. K. You gimme those books!

SALLY. Fat chance. You've been keeping two sets of books since you took over this place five years ago.

(to **TED**)

SALLY. *(cont.)* I found 'em layin' open on her desk. It's all here, Ted; everything the D.A. needs to put her away for a good long time.

(The **TEENS & KIDS** *cheer.)*

MRS. K. Now, now, children. Is that any way to treat your elders?

(Everyone cheers. **MRS. K.** *sits at the picnic table, defeated.)*

TED. Morty, tie her up somewhere. We all need a good night's sleep, and in the morning we'll load up the bus and get the heck out of here.

(puts the spark plugs in his pocket)

MORTY. Sounds good to me.

TED. And we should call their parents; let 'em know what's really going on and have 'em meet us over in Colesville. Ah, but the phones –

SALLY. – are working just fine. The lines are open now that the Orson Welles show is over. I phoned the story in to my editor and he's ripping up the second page for the morning edition.

IDA. Let's go, Elaine! We're tuckin' you in for the night.

*(***MORTY** *and* **IDA** *take* **MRS. K.** *by the arms towards the kitchen.)*

MRS. K. You won't get away with this!

TEENS & KIDS. Yes, we will!

MRS. K. No, you won't!

TEENS & KIDS. Yes, we will!

(This exchange continues, getting more childish, until **MORTY** *and* **IDA** *exit with* **MRS. K.** *into the kitchen.)*

#13: FINALE

(Music starts to underscore.)

CARL. Well, I guess we showed her, Mr. Connors.

TED. I think we pulled off the best Halloween prank that's ever been pulled.

JOAN. Next to Orson Welles.

SPARKY. But he had a whole studio of radio professionals. We just had us.

NANCY. Yeah, and it was fun.

SALLY. See what you can accomplish when you work as a team? Girls and boys CAN get along when they have to.

*(***TEENS & KIDS*** reluctantly ad-lib agreement.)*

SUSIE. Hey! What's that noise?

(Everyone becomes aware of some "spaceship noises" and green lights coming from somewhere. Two "alien" heads appear in the doorways and everyone turns front and sings,)

ALL.

WE GOTTA GET AWAY BEFORE THEY COME.
NO ONE HAS ANY IDEA WHAT WE'RE RUNNING FROM,
BUT WE ARE SAFE IN ASSUMIN' THEY'RE NOT EVEN HUMAN,
THOSE LITTLE GREEN MEN – FROM –

*(***MORTY*** and ***IDA*** enter through the doorways waving flashlights covered with a green cloth and holding alien masks. They laugh and everyone joins in.)*

HEY, HEY,
HAVIN' LOTS OF FUN SCARIN' EVERYONE.
WITCHES AND RATS AND VAMPIRE BATS APPEAR.
GOBLINS AND GHOULS AND MONSTERS THAT DROOL ARE
    HERE.
WE GET IN LATE AND PARENTS MIGHT HATE IT
BUT WE WAIT AND WAIT AND ANTICIPATE IT –

(**MRS. K.** *enters through the kitchen, tied with ropes to the large "Camp Gitchiegoomie" road sign where* **MORTY** *and* **IDA** *left her and she has pulled it out of the ground, insistent on being part of the Finale.*)

ALL. *(cont.)*

– ALL YEAR IN AND YEAR OUT WE ARE SO CRAZY – ABOUT HALLOWEEN –.

(blackout)

#14: CURTAIN CALL

#15: EXIT MUSIC

End of Act Two

PROPS, FURNITURE AND SET DRESSING

ACT ONE:
THE DINING HALL:
Onstage
Picnic table at C. (seats 4 on each side);
Empty camping plates, cups, utensils, dish towel on table;
Misc. crates, barrels, shelves w/ camping equipment, boxes in corners,
    along walls;
Army binoculars on one of the shelves;
Small table or large crate in one corner with "1938" radio on it,
    "plugged" into wall;
Curtains of plain fabric on wooden rods over windows;
Misc. animal head, Native American blankets, pelts and handmade
    Halloween decorations on walls;
Broom leaning in one corner;

Offstage
Tray with large "Halloween" cake on it;
Metal bucket or tub with a dozen red apples inside, hidden from view;
2 glasses of lemonade
Realistic animal hand puppets (see author's notes)
Wheel/tire and broken tailpipe from an old car
Empty marshmallow tin

THE CAMPFIRE:
Onstage
Campfire unit; small rocks and sticks over colored lights and gels; (self-
    powered by battery pack or connected by electrical cord to off-stage)
Low wooden benches or thick logs;
Several long thin sticks with marshmallows on the ends;
Several Native American blankets;

THE CABINS:
Onstage
Cots, sleeping bags, bunk beds as desired in each cabin;
The "1938" radio on a small table next to Susie's bed (or in it),
    "plugged" into the wall;
Curtains and bedsheets of distinct green colors, same fabrics used for
    "Martian costumes" in ACT II, Scene 2;
Wooden curtain rods above windows;
Misc. toys, pillows and blankets belonging to the campers;

Offstage
Several flashlights;
Misc. special effects for "Say Goodnight" dance sequence

ACT TWO:
THE CAMPFIRE:
Onstage
Same campfire unit and wooden benches as in ACT I;
OR: without these pieces, location can be another exterior area at the
     campsite;

Offstage
Animal hand puppets;

THE DINING HALL:
Onstage
Same as ACT I;

Offstage
Baseball bat
Car engine spark plugs
Toy accordion
Large beer stein
Plastic long-stem roses (Spanish dancers hold with teeth)
Serving tray with bottle of wine, glass, misc. snacks
Two large accountant's ledger books
Two "alien" masks
Coil of rope and large wooden "Camp Gitchiegoomie" road sign

COSTUME PLOT

TED CONNORS:

ACT I:

Rustic colored camp counselor uniform: ranger's hat, short sleeved workshirt with buttoned chest pockets, red neckerchief, peawhistle on a string around neck, long work pants and belt, dark socks and work shoes;

> Special for Scene 1: rubber flat-top Frankenstein head piece, (stick-on neck bolts, optional), tight-fitting old tweed sportcoat

ACT II: same as ACT I

> Special for Scene 2: "zoot" suit coat and hat, Swiss Tyrolian dancer; long wrap-around skirt and shawl for Spanish dancer;

SALLY DUNBAR:

ACT I:

Metropolitan stylish businesswoman's jacket and skirt (hat, gloves optional), hose, low-heeled shoes with one heel broken or loose;

> Special for Scene 3 thru end: brown moccasins to replace shoes;

ACT II: same as ACT I

Special for Scene 2: same as Ted above;

IDA ROTHBERG:

ACT I: same as above for TED:

> Special for Scene 1: "Bride of Frankenstein" wig and long white bedsheet as draped robe, open in back for quick removal;
>
> Special for Scene 4 thru end: frumpy woolen bathrobe, hairnet with curlers and fasteners, sleeping mask, baggy men's pajama top and bottom, moccasins or plain bedroom slippers;

ACT II: same as ACT I, Scene 4

> Special for Scene 2: same as Ted above, add long-braided blonde wig;

MORTY KLEIN:

ACT I:

White short order cook's cap or old NY Yankees baseball cap; wrinkled unwashed work shirt and pants; white short order cook's apron; dark socks and work shoes;

> Special for Scene 4 thru end: same as IDA above except for the hairnet and sleeping mask;

ACT II: same as ACT I, Scene 4

> Special for Scene 2: same as Ted above;

MRS. KOLOTSKY:
ACT I:
Dark plain mature woman's dress; eye glasses on a simple chain around neck; support hose and orthopedic shoes;

> Special for Scene 1: bright colored gypsy headscarf; spangly earrings, silk shawl, bright colored elastic-waisted peasant skirt;
> Special for Scene 4 thru ACT II, beginning of Scene 2: the Goblin costume: removable over-the-head monster mask and full body suit with easy-access front or back zipper or velcro; not a recognizable cartoon character or movie monster; not too scary for younger audiences;

ACT II: same as ACT I, Scene 3

CARL BENNETT:
ACT I:
Plain work shirt and pants; dark socks and work shoes;

> Special for Scene 1: home-made vampire costume: black cape, ornate cardboard medallion on ribbon around neck;
> Special for Scene 4: teen boy pajama top and bottom; white undershirt moccasins or plain bedroom slippers; (bathrobe or jacket, optional)

ACT II: same as ACT I, Scene 4

> Special for end of Scene 2: Martian costume; made from scrap fabrics and kitchen/garden utensils found around the camp: two-headed green full-length tunic with wrap around belt made from same fabrics as the curtains and bedsheets in the campers' cabins; utensils as mechanical hands; bent wire clothes hangers as antennae, etc.

SPARKY SCHULTZ:
ACT I:
Home-made jungle man outfit: red woolen longjohns, leopard skin tunic with one shoulder strap; white socks and work shoes;

> Special for Scene 4: same as Carl above

ACT II: same as ACT I, Scene 4

> Special for end of Scene 2: same as Carl above, sharing the two headed tunic;

JOAN McDOOGLE:
ACT I:
Boy's sailor outfit: white hat, large white or navy blue shirt, pants;
Socks, shoes;

> Special for Scene 4: same as Carl above;

ACT II: same as ACT, Scene 4

> Special for end of Scene 2: same as Carl above, sharing her two-headed tunic with Nancy;

NANCY GRIBBLE:
ACT I:

Hawaiian hula girl's costume: flowers in hair, colorful shirt, leis around
neck, wrap-around grass skirt, socks, shoes;

> Special for Scene 4: same as Carl above;

ACT II: same as ACT I, Scene 4;

> Special for end of Scene 2: same as Carl above, sharing the two-
> headed tunic with Joan;

JOEY DeLUCA:
ACT I:

Little Pirate captain: black hat with skull/crossbones, striped T-shirt,
(eyepatch optional), black pants, plastic sword and belt, dark socks
and shoes;

> Special for Scene 3: little Groom's costume; top hat, black tux,
> socks, shoes;

> Special for Scene 4: same as Carl above;

ACT II: same as ACT I, Scene 4;

> Special for end of Scene 2: green floor-length tunic, kitchen pot
> or bowl on head, bedroom slippers or knee-pads attached to
> knees so can walk on knees for several seconds;

GEORGIE JOHNSON:
ACT I:

Little Cowboy sheriff: hat, shirt and pants, sheriff's badge, toy gun and
holster, dark socks and shoes;

> Special for Scene 3: same as Joey above

> Special for Scene 4: same as Carl above;

ACT II: same as ACT I, Scene 4;

> Special for end of Scene 2: same as Joey above;

MARY GALE:
ACT I:

Little Witches' costume: pointy black hat, shawl, old baggy dress;
Dark socks and shoes;

> Special for Scene 3: little Bride's costume; white veil, dress;

> Special for Scene 4: same as Carl above;

ACT II: same as ACT I, Scene 4;

> Special for end of Scene 2: same as Joey above;

SUSIE SLAUSON:
ACT I:

Little Ballerina's costume: cheap tiara or ribbons in hair; full-body pink
leotard and frilly tutu; white tights; slippers;

> Special for Scene 3: same as Mary above

> Special for Scene 4: same as Carl above;

ACT II: same as ACT I, Scene 4;

> NOTE: does not wear a special Martian costume for end of
> Scene 2

SOUND CUES ON CD

I strongly recommend using the pre-recorded sound effects CD available with the music rental package. All of these tracks have been carefully edited from the original Orson Welles' WAR OF THE WORLDS radio broadcast to seamlessly fit in with the dialogue and action of the scenes without slowing down the suspense or energy of the performance. Highlights from the first 35 minutes of the original broadcast have been condensed to 5 minutes and accurately timed to keep your show moving briskly, thus saving you the time and expense of having to create your own sound cues. Trust me. Please use this CD for your production.

-Scott Martin

#1:   NIGHT SOUNDS; FROGS, CRICKETS; (ACT 1, SCENE 2)
          (begin at top of scene, fade out when desired before song)

#2:   RADIO STATIC AND MUSIC; (ACT 1, SCENE 3)
          (Susie turns on radio)

#3:   RADIO STATIC AND MUSIC; (ACT 1, SCENE 3)
          (Susie turns on radio; fade in and out under dialogue when desired)

#4   "CHARLIE McCARTHY SHOW;" (ACT 1, SCENE 4)
          (Susie turns on radio; fade in and out under business when desired)

#5 - #11: "WOTW" RADIO CUES (#1 - #7); (ACT 1, SCENE 4)

#12:   "WOTW" RADIO CUE (#8): (ACT II, SCENE 1)

#13:   RADIO STATIC AND MUSIC: (ACT II, SCENE 2)
          (Susie turns on radio; fade out when desired)

#14:   "WOTW" RADIO CUE (#9): (ACT II, SCENE 2)

#15:   SPACESHIP SOUNDS (ACT II, SCENE 2)

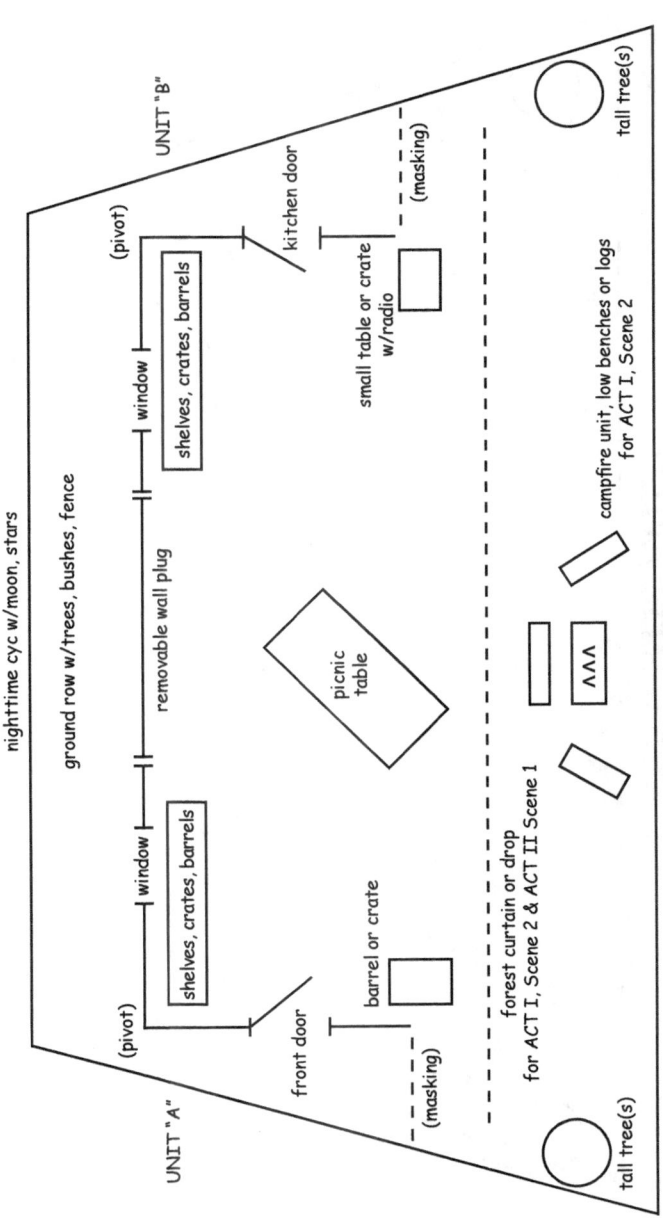

LITTLE GREEN MEN

DINING HALL/CAMPSITE

BASED ON AN ORIGINAL SET DESIGN BY TONY PERESLETE

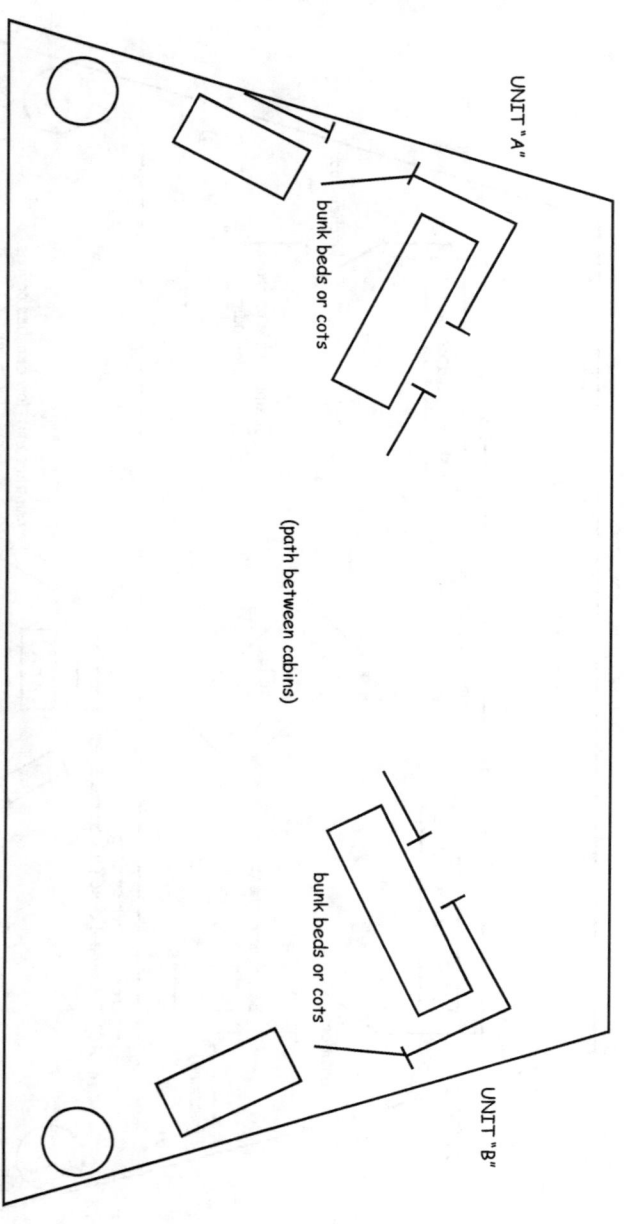

LITTLE GREEN MEN
TWO CABINS
BASED ON AN ORIGINAL SET DESIGN BY TONY PERESLETE

UNIT "A"

bunk beds or cots

(path between cabins)

bunk beds or cots

UNIT "B"

ABOUT THE PLAYWRIGHT

SCOTT MARTIN has worked extensively for many years in the Los Angeles area as an actor, director, writer, and musician. Among his many other successfully-produced musicals are: *Children of the Night* (the true story of author Bram Stoker's lifelong devotion to the great actor Sir Henry Irving), *Scream Queens – The Musical* (aging B-movie film actresses present a hilarious comedy revue for the fans at a horror and science fiction convention, also available from Samuel French), *Bleacher Babes* (the widows of a men's softball team reunite for one last picnic), as well as such family-friendly parodies as *Rockin' Robin Hood, The Road to Paradise, The Maltese Chicken,* and *Darn Dodgers.* He has written material for numerous revues and industrial shows, film projects and children's theatre productions, and is a long-time member of ASCAP. For more information visit www.scottmartinmusicals.com